Tek Power

Also by William Shatner

Tek Secret
Tek Vengeance
TekLab
TekLords
TekWar

Tek Power

WILLIAM SHATNER

An Ace/Putnam Book
Published by G. P. Putnam's Sons
New York

An Ace/Putnam Book
Published by G. P. Putnam's Sons
Publishers Since 1838
200 Madison Avenue
New York, NY 10016

Library of Congress Cataloging-in-Publication Data
Shatner, William.
Tek power / William Shatner.
p. cm.
ISBN 0-399-13997-4
1. Cardigan, Jake (Fictitious character)—Fiction.—2. Private
investigators—Fiction. I. Title.
PS3569.H347T415   1994   94-16649/ CIP
813'.54—dc20

Printed in the United States of America
2   3   4   5   6   7   8   9   10

This book is printed on acid-free paper.
∞

And the drums keep beating . . .
And the books keep coming . . .
And Tek continues to multiply.

*From a modest beginning in October 1989 to
now, the tidal wave that is Tek contains six novels, twenty-four
comic books, four movies, and now, the Holy Grail of popular
literature, a* TekWar *television series on the USA Network.*

*Obeisance must be paid to Ron Goulart, Carmen LaVia, Susan
Allison, Mary Jo Fernandez, Ivy Fischer Stone, and to
Sterling and Martika, my two Dobies, who have guarded the
Tek books and have a couple of dog-eared copies
themselves.*

Tek Power

1

□

HIS LIFE CHANGED for good and all on a stormy night in the summer of the year 2121. A vidphone call began the process.

It was a few minutes short of midnight in Secure Zone 2 of Manhattan when the phone in Richard Bascom's tower-apartment bedroom buzzed harshly.

Out beyond the wide blanked windows of the room lightning crackled. Thunder seemed to be rolling along the rainswept pedestrian ramps and streets out there in the night.

A lanky, sandyhaired man in his middle thirties, Richard hadn't yet fallen asleep. Sitting up in the oval bed, he said, "Lights."

As the room filled with soft light, he nodded toward the small vidphone screen resting on the floating bedside table. "I'll take the call."

The rectangular screen whirred faintly as it turned to face him. But it remained blank. "Listen, old buddy," came a slurred male voice.

Richard didn't recognize it. "Who is this?"

"Just pay attention," continued the unseen caller. "No matter what they try to tell you—she was murdered."

"Who was murdered?" Swinging his legs off the bed, Richard stood up. "What the hell are you talking about?"

"Eve, old buddy. I'm talking about your loyal, loving wife." The phone clicked off.

He frowned at the dead phone. "Jesus, has something happened to Eve?"

Turning on his heel and grabbing up his robe, he went running from the room.

The high, wide window of their apartment living room hadn't been blanked. A sudden blaze of bluish lightning showed him the towering apartment houses out there, the rainy pedramps and the flitting skycars, as he hurried to Eve's bedroom.

His wife went out on a dinner date with some client or other tonight, but he'd assumed she had long since come home.

She hadn't, though. Her bedroom was empty, the oval bed neatly made, just as the servobot had left it this morning.

His frown deepening, Richard glanced around the room. He had no idea what he was expecting to see. Her memopad screen was sitting on a low table, but he had no way to access it.

"A practical joke," he decided. "Sure, that damn call was just a practical joke."

Eve wasn't dead.

"That guy sounded as though he was drunk or high on something. A Tekhead maybe, who believes in his hallucinations."

Eve wasn't dead. Couldn't be.

The thing to do was find out whom she'd gone to dinner with and where.

"Problem is," he said to himself while he wandered around his wife's silent bedroom, "Eve hasn't been all that confiding lately."

He had no idea where she'd gone this evening. Not only that, he wasn't even sure which person at Larson-Dunn, the public relations outfit Eve worked for, he could call to ask for information.

"Is Terry Wollter still with L-D? Seems to me she mentioned he was fired couple months back."

Wollter was just about the only one at the firm he knew well enough to contact at this hour.

He sat on the edge of her bed. He'd pulled the robe on over his pajamas, yet he was feeling extremely cold. He clenched his fists to keep himself from shaking.

Eve wasn't dead.

It had to be a joke. Some damned drunk, some Tekkie with a sense of humor.

Funny how thorough the servobot had been. There was hardly a trace of Eve left in the bedroom. It was chill and smelled faintly antiseptic. The sandalwood perfume she usually wore wasn't discernible at all.

Richard got up, slowly, and made his way into the living room. "But where is she?" he said, stopping near the window. "Where the hell is she?"

The heavy rain kept slamming down through the night. Everything out there was blurred, looking as though it might melt away at any moment.

"Okay, I'll wait another fifteen minutes," he decided. "Then I'll get in touch with Wollter."

Even if the guy no longer worked at Larson-Dunn, he ought to know somebody who could tell him where Eve had gone tonight.

Richard told himself, not for the first time, that he was going to have to work harder on his relationship with his wife. "Lately things haven't been going—"

"Sir?" came the soft, polite voice of the apartment computer.

He turned to glance up at the grey overhead voxbox. "Yes, what?"

"There's someone at the pedramp entrance, sir," announced the computer.

"Who?"

"Two people, actually, who identify themselves as members of the Manhattan Police Service," replied the slightly metallic voice. "I'm afraid, sir, that your wife has suffered an accident."

JAKE CARDIGAN WAS, he decided, in pretty good shape. "For a guy who's getting ever closer to fifty," he added.

Twilight was slowly spreading across the Malibu Sector of Greater Los Angeles and Jake was running, alone, along a stretch of beach that led to the apartment he shared with his son. He'd done two miles out and was now heading for home.

He kept up a steady pace, not winded at all.

The surf was relatively quiet tonight, the foam came whispering in across the wet sand.

Trotting along the water's edge, coming in Jake's direction, was a highly polished chromeplated robot. He was holding the glowing fiberoptic leashes of two listless peppermint poodles.

"Bon soir," greeted the bot as he and the two dogs passed Jake.

"Evening. Where's the third one?"

"Un peu mal," replied the robot.

Nodding sympathetically, Jake continued on his run.

Up ahead on his right loomed a brightly illuminated beach house, only a few months old, built of glittering metal struts and large curved panels of tinted plastiglass. Out on the glowing neo-wood sundeck about thirty people were gathered, talking and drinking. On the small holostage at the far side of the deck a projected string quartet was playing chamber music that didn't match the look of the party.

Spotting Jake passing, a plump pretty blonde in a tight yellow slaxsuit hurried over to the beachside railing and waved. "Jake, hey," she called. "Didn't you get my invitation, hon?"

He slowed his pace but didn't stop completely. "Can't make the festivities, Maggie," he shouted. "Sorry."

"We're going to have fun." Maggie brought up her clenched fist from her side and opened it for a few seconds. She was holding what looked to be a Tek chip.

Sudden anger hit Jake, but he only gave her a thin grin and a farewell wave. "So I see." Kicking up his pace, he soon left the party behind.

He'd been jogging along for about another ten minutes when he heard a muffled cry from up near an unlit beach house some three hundred feet inland from him.

Jake slowed again, then halted to scan the shadows beneath the place.

It was one of several plastiglass and simulated redwood stilt-houses that had been built along here back in the early 2100s.

Nodding to himself, Jake sprinted up across the sand. "What are you lads up to?" he called.

He'd spotted two bulky figures struggling with a smaller, slimmer figure.

Two large thickset young men were assaulting an auburn-haired young woman. The largest had an armlock on her and was trying to get her shoulder bag free of her grasp.

"Keep on jogging, asshole," the other lout advised Jake. Letting go of the struggling woman's arm, he spun to glower at him.

Jake kicked out, hard, connecting with his kneecap. He followed that with three jabs to the young man's fat chin.

The lunk made a few unhappy grunting noises before dropping to the sandy ground.

Jake took hold of the second lout by the back of his laminated shirt and yanked. Spinning him around, he delivered two effective punches to his sagging midsection and another to his left temple as he doubled up.

The huge youth said, "Oof—ung," and then toppled to his knees.

When Jake booted him in the backside, he fell all the way over and spilled out next to his unconscious companion.

Jake turned to the young woman. "Did they—Hey! Alicia Bower."

"Hi, Jake." She brushed at the front of her skirt as she moved nearer to him. "Excuse me for barging in on you like this."

He walked her a few yards downhill toward the darkening sea.

He asked, "You were coming to see me?"

Alicia nodded, smiling faintly. "I happened to be flying over Malibu, trying out my new skyvan, when I remembered that you lived in the vicinity," she explained. "So I decided to set down at a public lot up the way." She indicated its direction with a half swing of her left shoulder. "I was strolling over to pay you a visit when I got jumped by those two burly muggers."

"Yeah?"

She held up her right hand. "Yes, honestly," she assured him. "I haven't, afterall, seen you since you extricated me from that mess in Farmland and helped me get my brains unscrambled.''

Jake looked her slowly up and down. "You don't, you know, need an elaborate excuse to pay me a visit," he told her. "You didn't rig this show, did you?"

"No, most certainly not." She held out her slim right arm. "I wouldn't pay those goons to give me these bruises, would I?"

He glanced up into the thickening dark around the stilthouse. The pair of attackers had revived and were stumbling rapidly away in the opposite direction. He ignored them, saying to the young woman, "Okay, I believe you—for now. How have you been?"

"Isn't the complete phrase 'How have you been, little girl?' " Anger tinged her voice. "I'm twenty-seven and, as you should know, not particularly innocent."

"I often ask my friends how they've been," he said. "Even those who aren't little girls. In this part of the country that sort of inquiry isn't an insult."

"Allright, sorry. I'm still somewhat edgy around you," Alicia admitted. "But after what we went through together—I don't know, I thought I'd hear from you after you got me safely home."

"Sometimes I send out cheery faxgrams to my former clients during the holiday season."

She rested her fists on her narrow hips. "I'm not easily dissuaded," she informed him. "Maybe you didn't get the impression when you were springing me from that booby hatch back in Farmland, but I'm damned stubborn." She paused to take a slow breath in. "Would you like to go to dinner with me?"

"Sometime?"

"No, damn it," she said impatiently. "Now, tonight. That's one of the things I dropped by to ask you."

He grinned, nodding. "Sure," he said. "There's a pretty good seafood café about a half mile back along the beach. We can hike there if you're up to it."

"Of course I am. It sounds fine." She took hold of his arm and they started walking. "Don't you stay friendly with people you've met while working on a case?"

He watched the dark ocean. Far out the colored lights of a lone hoverboat were flashing. "Once in a while."

2

"WRONG SCREEN," apologized the lean plainclothes policeman. "Sorry."

He and Richard Bascom were down in the monitor room of the Manhattan Municipal Morgue and one of the dozen large vidscreens built into the circular wall had just come to life.

Richard saw two blood-splattered white medibots performing an autopsy on the body of a dead child.

Detective Busino said, "No need to look at that." Reaching out to the wall control pad, he shut off the screen and the noise of the surgical saw. "You okay, sir?"

Richard slapped his hand against the nearest metal wall to steady himself. "More or less," he answered in a voice that didn't sound like his own to him. "Is there any way to turn up the heat down here?"

"No, afraid not. It's controlled from upstairs." The cop poked again at the control pad. "Would you, please, take a look at Screen 11?"

"Which?"

"Behind you."

He turned and saw a new image. The body of a dead woman was stretched out on a white metal table, partially covered with a thin white plyosheet. The body was battered, twisted and broken, one whole side of the face was a crusty black. All his breath seemed to sigh out of him as he realized he was staring at Eve.

Two white medibots, arms at their sides, were standing next to the table that held the sad remains of his wife.

Richard brought his other hand up to his face, covering his eyes for a moment. Then he dropped his hand and straightened up. "Are those damn gadgets going . . . going to cut her up?"

"No, sir, no," Detective Busino assured him. "Now I need you to tell me positively that this is your wife."

"Yes, that's Eve," he said quietly. "But don't I get to see her? In the same room, I mean, so I can touch her."

"Afraid you can't do that, not at this stage anyway," the officer told him. "This is definitely Eve Scanlon Bascom?"

"Yes, yeah, it is—do we have to keep looking at her?"

"No, course not." Busino turned off the screen. "Some people like to watch long as they can."

Richard crossed to one of the three white metal chairs across the round room. "Am I allowed to sit?"

"Sure."

"What happened to her?"

The detective put his hands in his trouser pockets and leaned against the wall. "Your wife's skycar was rerouted because—"

"She was alone in her car?"

"Yes, alone. You thought she was with someone?"

"She was having dinner with a client. I wasn't sure if—"

"Only your wife was in the vehicle," he said. "She had been passing over Secure Zone 1 and then she was rerouted over Danger Zone 3."

"Why? That was a—"

"Couldn't be helped. As you probably know, President Brookmeyer was visiting Manhattan tonight. And when the President of the United States is traveling over Secure Zone 1 in his skycade, all other traffic is automatically diverted elsewhere. Standard procedure."

"What happened?"

"Just a chance thing," he replied. "That's how life goes sometimes. While she was traveling over Danger Zone 3, a stolen skyvan smashed into her. Couple of Tekhead punks out joyriding. They died, too."

Richard asked him, "You're certain this was an accident?"

"Absolutely." Busino took his hands from his pockets. "Unless you have something to tell me that'll maybe change our minds."

"No, nothing." He stood up and discovered he was a little unsteady on his feet. "Is there a vidphone I can use?"

"Out in Corridor 3." The detective came over and took hold of his arm. "I'll show you, sir."

"Thanks."

"These things happen," he said as he helped him toward the door. "It's just chance, fate. Nothing you can do about it."

"Maybe," said Richard quietly, "there is something I can do."

DARKNESS HAD LONG since closed in around Captain Noah's Café. The Pacific Ocean out beyond the domecovered dining deck was a velvety black.

"Her name is Kay Norwood," Alicia was saying, both elbows resting on the tabletop. "A longtime friend of mine—one of the few, actually, that I have left—and an absolutely terrific corporate lawyer."

"I've heard of her."

"Kay's been doing a great job of helping me get my father's estate straightened out." She laughed, shaking her head. "The affairs of Mechanix International are really screwed up, Jake. My dear departed dad was in cahoots with all sorts of scoundrels—crooks, Teklords and a wide variety of government sneaks."

Jake asked her, "Are you going to be, do you think, controlling the operation eventually?"

"You bet your ass I am," she assured him. "We're going to dump all the doinks and deadheads. Roger Zangerly is helping out, too. He's one of the few Mechanix execs I can halfway trust."

"And what about Barry Zangerly?"

"We aren't," she said, spreading her fingers wide and studying them, "living together anymore."

Jake said nothing.

"But I'm not going back to my old promiscuous ways," she added. "I'm living alone—without even a servobot to help out—at my father's Palisades Sector home."

"Big place to inhabit alone."

"You've been there, haven't you?"

"Once—briefly."

"That's right, you were lured there and—"

"Lured is too polite a word to describe it," he put in. "I was out-and-out dumb and let myself get conned. I almost got trounced as a result."

"My fault that was."

He grinned. "Nope, entirely mine."

"Well, you'd been hired to find me." She leaned back in her chair. "Hired by Barry actually. I feel badly about abandoning him. But I really think it's important to be by myself for a while."

"Thanks for letting me intrude on your solitude tonight."

"You're one of the exceptions." Alicia blinked, sitting up. "Oh, you were teasing me, weren't you? Am I starting to sound self-important and soulful?"

"Just a mite."

"I'll quit," she promised. "Tell me what you're working on now—if it's not confidential."

"At the moment I'm between cases."

Resting her elbows on the table again, Alicia said, "I've been thinking I'd like to see you now and then. In a strictly friendship sort of way."

"I'm pretty much practicing the solitary life myself these days," he told her. "As far as any sort of social life goes."

She said, "I suppose I'm making too much of the fact that you saved my life."

"That was part of my job," he said. "What you have to understand, Alicia, is that any one of a dozen other Cosmos Detective Agency operatives could've—"

"Excessive modesty doesn't fit you very well." She gave a shake of her head. "I'm not a schoolgirl and this isn't a crush. I like *you*—Jake Cardigan. If we'd met at a party or a brawl, I'd still think of you as an exceptional person."

"An exceptional person who's nearly twice your age."

She laughed. "Is that what's bothering you? You don't want to get involved with a kid?"

Jake studied the black starless sky up above the restaurant deck. "It's simpler than that," he answered finally. "I don't want to get involved with anybody, age has very little to—"

"Excuse me, *amigo,* for intruding on what sounds like it's bound to develop into a very touching spiel—and how might you be, Miss Bower." Gomez had come striding out onto the deck. He bowed toward the young woman. "We've never met, *señorita,* but no doubt you've heard of me. Sid Gomez, Jake's partner and wellknown ace detective in my own right."

Eyeing him, Jake inquired, "You just happen to be passing by, too?" He indicated the third chair with a tilt of his thumb.

Gomez was a dark curlyhaired man, about ten years younger than his partner. He remained standing. "When I checked with Dan at your residence, he informed me you'd reported in that you were cavorting here."

"So what's happening?"

"Walt Bascom, our esteemed *jefe,* wants to see us immediately if not sooner. He awaits at the Cosmos Detective Agency building."

"I'll have to go, Alicia." He pushed back from the table. "We'll escort you to your skycar."

"Thanks, I'd feel safer if you did." Standing, she held out her hand to Gomez. "Nice to meet you. I've heard a good deal about you."

He bent, kissed her hand. *"Sí,* I'm a legend in my own time."

Jake stood. "Must be an important case Bascom has for us."

As the three of them crossed the deck, Gomez said, "I don't know exactly what's going on, since the chief hasn't as yet provided any details. I have the feeling, though, that there's something special about this one."

3

JAKE NODDED AT the figure that had materialized atop the holo-gram projection stage. "That's your son, isn't it?"

"One of them," answered Bascom. "Richard, the youngest." The agency head was sitting, somewhat stiffly, behind his large desk. "Lives in New York." His desktop was uncharacteristically uncluttered. "He works for the TriState EdSystem as a Lit professor." All the windows in the big tower office had been blanked and nothing of the night streets of this part of the Malibu Sector showed. "Until tonight he was married."

"And what happened tonight, *jefe?*" Gomez was sitting on the edge of the holostage with part of Richard Bascom's left foot superimposed on his backside.

Bascom, whose grey suit was considerably rumpled, reached out to the control panel again. "His wife was killed." The figure of a slender darkhaired woman of about thirty replaced the image of the detective agency head's son. "Eve was her name."

Standing up and away from the platform, Gomez asked, "Didn't she work for some public relations outfit?"

"Yeah, for Larson-Dunn." Bascom touched the controls again and Eve vanished. "Their Manhattan office."

Jake was straddling a straightback metal chair. "A very shifty outfit," he commented, "and not one known for its probity."

"Both Larson and Dunn are corrupt, moneygrubbing swine," said Bascom. "Their organization's been involved in numerous shady deals both domestic and foreign."

Gomez had roamed over to one of the high wide blanked windows. He tapped absently on the plastiglass with his forefinger. "How would you rate Eve's honesty and integrity?"

"Not very highly."

Jake said, "Did your son share your opinion?"

"Nope, not at all."

"Ever discuss it with—"

"Only once. That was three years or so ago. Right before he went and married her," said Bascom. "I'd already heard a little something about the lady, and that public relations gang she was working for. Larson-Dunn has its headquarters office in Washington, DC, and I've had a few run-ins with them. They tend to represent scoundrels in the business, political and criminal areas—crooked tycoons, Teklords, bloodstained dictators and the like."

"You know for a fact that Eve herself was crooked?"

"Hell, she'd have to be to sign up with that bunch in the first place," answered the chief. "And, although I never told Richard about this, I had the lady checked out."

"Remind me in future incarnations," said Gomez, "not to have a gumshoe for a relative."

"How much of what you found out about her did you pass along to your son?"

"Not a hell of a lot, Jake. Richard and I—well, we haven't been all that close for a long time," admitted Bascom. "So I only hinted that maybe he ought to wait, look into her background a little more."

"I bet that didn't work too well."

"He told me to go screw myself and hung up. We didn't talk to each other again for nearly a year."

Jake asked, "Have you kept checking up on her?"

Bascom sighed. "Yep, I have every so often," he said slowly. "In addition to dealing with a slew of extremely fragrant clients here and abroad, Eve has been—Eve was not particularly faithful to my son."

"How much so?"

"Oh, she wasn't exactly promiscuous, but she carried on several affairs after she married my son."

"Muy mal," commented Gomez as he settled into an armchair.

The image of a blond, overweight man of forty materialized on the stage. "This lad was the most recent of her lovers. Arnold Maxfield, Jr."

"Son of the communications mogul," said Jake.

Gomez sat up. "Didn't Junior get knocked off in some sort of accident down Nicaragua way only last week?"

"Might be it wasn't an accident," said Bascom. "I'm sorry I didn't put fulltime operatives on Eve soon as I heard about Maxfield's death."

"Was she with him down there, *jefe?*"

"Supposedly Eve was in Managua on Larson-Dunn business for nearly two weeks. He was down there at the same time and the day after she headed for home, Maxfield was killed during a riot at an air soccer match," he told them. "She and Junior saw a lot of each other, day *and* night."

Jake rubbed his knuckles across his cheek. "How was she killed and where?"

"Back in New York City—at roughly eleven PM tonight—when a runaway skyvan slammed into her skycar."

"Two fatal accidents in a week," observed Gomez, "make for a nice coincidence."

"At midnight, before he even knew anything had happened, Richard got a call," continued the chief. "The caller was a man and he kept the screen blanked. He told my son, in what sounds to me like a nasty way, that no matter what anybody tried to tell him, his wife had been murdered."

"Be interesting," said Jake, "to find out what that guy knows."

"I've already had an op with your Manhattan affiliate trying to track down the call." Bascom shook his head. "Made from a booth in a skybus station."

"You want us to head back to New York?"

"I've already booked you both on a skyliner that leaves GLA at two AM this morning."

Standing up, Gomez asked, "How many sons do you have?"

"Three, and I'd like very much to have all of them attend my wake someday," he said. "I wouldn't want Richard to have an accident." He placed both hands, palms down, on the uncluttered desk top. "He and I don't get along too damn well, but when this came up—and after the cops told him her death was an accident plain and simple—he turned to me for help. I'm glad he did and I don't want him feeling that I let him down."

"We'll give him the same matchless service we provide all our clients," promised Gomez. "With a few added frills to boot."

"If you could avoid it, fellas," cautioned Bascom, "don't tell him anything about his wife's romances. Okay?"

"WHAT YOU NEED is somebody who's not a lunatic." Dan Cardigan, a lean young man of sixteen, was leaning in the doorway of his father's bedroom and watching him pack.

"Alicia's actually a stable and rational person," Jake told his son. "You, like the lady herself, tend to believe all the rumors you've heard about her."

"From what you tell me, she just about came stalking you tonight."

"All she did was pay me a friendly social call."

"So are you going to start dating her?"

"Wasn't planning to, no."

Dan said, "Still, you ought to be dating someone."

"Eventually." He shut the single suitcase he was planning to take.

"What's wrong with Bev Kendricks?"

"Not a damn thing, far as I know."

"I figured, after you ran into her while you were working on that case involving Alicia Bower, that you'd renew your old friendship."

"What Bev and I had back when we were both cops wasn't exactly a friendship." He lifted the suitcase off his bed.

"But she's a private eye now, too, just like you. That sure as hell gives you something in common."

"Too much probably."

Dan took a few steps backward. "I'm not trying to play matchmaker, Dad. But, you know, I hate to see you turning into a recluse."

"I get around too much to be ranked a recluse." He carried the suitcase out into the hallway.

"Any idea how long you'll be back East?"

"Few days at least. And I've got a feeling this one could lead us pretty far afield."

"Have you ever met Bascom's son?"

"Nope."

"How do they get along?"

"Not, according to Bascom, very well," answered Jake. "Mainly because he tried to intrude into his son's personal life. A bad practice."

"Ah, I see the parallel you're attempting to make, Pops." He walked alongside his father to the door of the apartment.

"I always suspected you were a perceptive kid."

Dan laughed. "Maybe you'll meet an interesting woman in New York."

"New York is a vast metropolis. Bound to be several interesting women residing thereabouts."

Dan put his hand on Jake's shoulder. "Excuse the paternalistic attitude," he said, "but I do worry about you."

The door announced, "There's a Gomez on the doorstep."

The small vidscreen mounted in the door's midsection showed them a picture of the moustached detective.

"Ready to embark, *amigo?*" inquired Gomez's image.

"Be right there." Turning, Jake hugged his son.

4

HE SHOULDN'T HAVE lost his temper, since he was, afterall, only arguing with a robot. But Nathan Anger kept growing increasingly upset and found himself yelling at the smug, goddamned silvery mechanical man. "You've got to *stop* this, Sunny," he shouted, his hands fisting and his breathing starting to get choppy. "It draws too much attention to—"

"You're the one, jocko, who's going to attract attention. Especially with all these little tantrums of yours." The big silverplated bot was lounging, crosslegged, in a padded plastiglass rocker at the center of the big oval living room.

It was nearly three AM and a light, steady rain was falling all across New Baltimore. You could hear the unvaried patter of it on the domed ceiling of their topfloor condo.

Anger, wrapped in a thin black nightrobe, was pacing back and forth in front of the simulated fireplace. *"You* take orders from *me,"* he reminded, struggling to control his voice and to keep the rage he was feeling from breaking through.

"That's your notion, not mine."

"I'm the one who's a top agent with the Office of Clandestine Operations," he reminded. "You, Sunny, work for me and—"

"People who go out of their way to tell you they're top agents usually aren't."

The short, compact agent took a few quick breaths in and out. "A cat, for Christ sake."

"It annoyed me, jocko."

"Nothing's supposed to *annoy* you. You're a goddamn *machine.*"

"A top machine in my field."

"You're a bodyguard, an enforcer, an interrogator," said Anger. "You're not supposed to make a decision about anything."

"I've saved your ass more than once by making a quick sizeup of a situation."

"Killing somebody's pet—Jesus, breaking its damn neck—that's completely nuts."

"Machines can't go nuts, can they? Not according to your theory."

"It wasn't bad enough you kill the thing. No, then you leave it tossed out there in the condo courtyard. If I hadn't spotted it before Mrs. Averil got a look at—"

"It was a nasty caterwauling nuisance," observed Sunny. "Much better off dead."

"Doing stuff like that is—damn it, it's not tactful."

The robot made a harsh snickering sound. "That's very funny, jocko," he said. "We can kill Eve Bascom and that's perfectly okay. But get rid of some pissant feline and—"

"*We* didn't kill Eve Bascom."

"Right, we only helped arrange it."

"That's a very different thing."

Sunny leaned back in his chair and spread his glittering metal hands wide. "You're hairsplitting again."

"The point is, you've got to control these violent impulses of yours," Anger told him. "Otherwise, I'm going to haul you into the OCO offices and order a complete—"

"You won't do that."

"Oh, won't I now?"

Sunny made a chuckling noise. "It wouldn't be at all smart," he advised. "I know too much about you. No, you don't want to risk annoying me."

The lefthand pocket of Anger's dark robe buzzed. Scowling, he yanked out the palmsize phone. "Who?"

"Access A2," said the phone.

Anger sat down on the low black sofa. "I'll take it."

A husky black man appeared on the tiny rectangular screen. "How come we haven't had any further followup reports on the Eve Bascom matter?"

"I was about to contact you, when I got distracted by another matter," the OCO agent apologized.

"Distracted by a kitty." Sunny snickered again.

When the tapping sounded on the metal door of his small sky-liner compartment, Jake said, "C'mon in, Sid."

His partner, wearing a very bright orange robe, crossed the threshold from the adjoining compartment. "Have I grown several feet in height since we departed Greater LA?"

"Not noticeably, no."

"Then my room really is as squatty as I thought." He was carrying a laptop filescreen. "Finding myself in a sleepless state, I've been going over again this background stuff Bascom passed on to us." He settled into the room's other chair. "Haven't you been sleeping either?"

"Nope." Jake was still dressed.

"Is something other than this case bothering you?"

"I was thinking about what Dan said tonight."

"Doesn't pay to heed what any near relative has to say. Most of my earlier wives, for example, were notoriously crack-brained."

"My son was suggesting that I'm turning into a recluse—not literally but in a social sense."

"Tell him you've been losing yourself in your work. That's a perfectly acceptable USA pastime."

"Beth Kittridge has been dead for several months," he said quietly. He unblanked the small oval compartment window and looked out into the night sky they were rushing through.

"Some things," said Gomez, "take quite a lot of time to get over."

"I'm probably taking way too long."

Gomez shrugged one shoulder. "What do you think?"

"I still miss her," answered Jake. "I've accepted, you know, the fact she's dead and out of my life for the rest of my days." He watched the darkness again for a moment. "I don't know, Sid. There just hasn't been anyone since Beth."

"She was an exceptional lady," said his partner. "Women like that you usually don't find more than once per given lifetime. Unfortunate, but that's one of the annoying ground rules of life."

"I'm also a little uneasy about Alicia's looking me up," he admitted. "She's an interesting young woman, but what I feel about her is more avuncular than romantic."

"I don't think she's the kind of *mujer* who'll keep tossing herself at you."

Jake said, "Could be this is a symptom of growing older. I'm losing interest in romantic affairs."

"No es verdad. You never lose interest," Gomez assured him.

Jake said, "Enough about the life and loves of Jake Cardigan."

Gomez said, "I've been going over this list of *hombres* that Eve Bascom had a fling with."

"And?"

"Well, one thing I'm wondering is why Ricardo didn't tumble to what was afoot. There were nine different gents since they were married. Nine the chief found out about—there may be a few more who escaped the tally. You'd have to do some serious looking the other way to miss noticing your wife carrying on with close on to a dozen guys."

"Some people don't want to notice."

"Seems *muy tonto* to me."

"We can ask Richard about it—very carefully," said Jake. "Bascom's anxious we don't tell his son anything about his wife that he doesn't already know."

"Sooner or later sonny's going to find out." Gomez smoothed an end of his moustache. "Suppose, for instance, that her death does have some connection with Junior Maxfield's demise? If we establish that, he's going to realize they were up to something besides diplomacy down there."

"He may already suspect that and just didn't mention it to his father."

Tapping the filescreen, Gomez said, "After we talk to the boss's son and get all the background stuff from him we can, we're probably going to have to check out every single fellow on this list of Eve's old beaux."

Jake nodded. "A sad business," he said.

THIS TIME HE'D be able to do something.

Jake got to Berlin ahead of her. It was a cold, grey morning filled with heavy rain. A small crowd was already gathering on the rainslick street in front of the World Drug Court. They huddled beneath dark umbrellas, curious onlookers, watching the long passway that led from the curb to the narrow gate of the court building.

There were ten armed guards, human and robot, strung out on each side of the passway.

Then the landcar pulled up, the one carrying Beth and the International Drug Control Agency men assigned to escort her safely into the trial to testify.

Things were going to be okay. This time he'd be able to do something. This time Beth wasn't going to die.

Jake started to push his way through the growing crowd. The man nearest him turned out to be Bascom.

"Easy, Jake, don't shove."

"But they're going to attempt to kill her." He started to push around him.

"I have another case for you to work on." Rain was rolling down off his black umbrella and hitting at Jake's face. "Much more important than this one."

"Damn you, get out of my way."

A few feet away he saw another Jake. This one called out to

Beth, grinned, waved his hand. "Thought for a while I wasn't going to make it."

"Jake!" A smile brightened her face and she pulled herself free of the IDCA agent who was holding her arm. "My god, where've you been?"

Jake shouted, cupping his hands. "That's not me, Beth! It's a kamikaze—an android loaded with explosives!"

She didn't seem to hear him. She kept moving toward the false Jake.

An agent was trotting after her, reaching out to pull her back.

Jake fought to get near. "Beth, no!" he yelled. "I know what's going to happen."

The other Jake, grinning, held out his arms to her.

She put her arms tight around the android. "I'm so glad—"

There was an enormous explosion.

"No!" cried Jake. "I have to save you."

The rain turned blood red and came slamming at him. It knocked him to the sidewalk, pounding at his chest.

"How you doing, *amigo?*"

Jake sat up on his narrow bed. "Sid?"

"You were hollering," explained his partner from the compartment doorway. "I thought I'd best pop in."

"Thanks, but it's nothing," Jake assured him. "A bad dream. Can't even remember what it was about."

"It was about Beth."

"Naw, I don't think—"

"I heard you shouting her name over and over."

Jake sighed and nodded his head slowly. "Yeah, I go back to Berlin quite a lot," he admitted. "Most often I get another chance to try to save her. But, shit, I never succeed. Just like in real life." He hit at his leg with his fist. "If I hadn't been such an asshole, letting myself get sidetracked in Brazil—Beth would be alive."

"It's over and done," said Gomez. "Like everything else that's ever happened up until just now, it's in the past. Let it go, Jake."

"I'm trying," he said. "I'll be okay now—get some sleep."

Gomez turned away. "You, too, *amigo.*"

5

□

THE NEW DAY had already started, the night completely faded away, by the time Richard had returned to his apartment. He stood in the living room, hands thrust deep into the pockets of his outercoat, staring out into the morning and yet seeing nothing.

"It's too cold in here," he said aloud after a moment.

"I'll raise the temperature, sir," responded the voice of the computer obligingly. "Is that better?"

"What?"

"I've elevated the temperature."

"Yeah, okay." Keeping his coat on and his hands in his pockets, Richard sat on the bright crimson sofa. He was shivering, his teeth clicking.

"There have been some vidphone messages, sir," the computer informed him after a moment.

"I'll listen later." He leaned back. That didn't feel especially comfortable. He sat up again.

Concentrating on the big wide window, he forced himself to take in the view outside in the grey morning. A skycab was drifting slowly by; a chubby young woman in a plyo running suit was jogging along the Level 18 pedramp; a robot doorman, decked out in a crimson-and-gold uniform, was taking his position in front of the private hotel across the way.

"Life goes on," muttered Richard, "as Detective Busino would say."

"Sir?"

"Nothing, I'm babbling to myself. Ignore it."

"Might I," ventured the computer after another moment had passed, "inquire as to Mrs. Bascom's condition?"

"She's dead. That's her condition."

"Oh." A concerned gasp came out of the overhead voxbox. "I'm terribly sorry, sir. Is there anything I can—"

"No, not a damn thing right now." He stood up. "Who phoned, did you say?"

"Your father, a reporter from Newz, Mrs. Truett and Dean Allen of the Lit Department."

He crossed to a chair that faced the vidwall. "I'd like to see my dad's message."

"Right away, sir."

Walt Bascom was behind his desk, hands folded. "This is to update you, son, on what's going on," he said. "I've arranged to have operatives from the Continental Detective Agency, which is our chief affiliate back that way, set up an around-the-clock security watch on you. I know you don't think it's necessary, but I—"

"I don't, but, hell, I'll go along with it. I ran into one of those ops just now in the hall."

". . . Cardigan and Sid Gomez will be arriving in Manhattan this morning," Bascom's message was continuing. "They'll be contacting you. These lads, especially Jake, tend to annoy people and rub them the wrong way. But they're among the best detectives we have and they almost always get results. I'll—"

The wall went suddenly black.

"How the hell'd you guys get in here?" Springing up from his chair, Richard faced the two men showing in the doorway. "Who let you in?"

The computer, too, had fallen silent.

One of the men was small, only a shade over five feet high. He had a completely bald head that seemed at least a few sizes too large for him. In his knobby left hand was gripped a pearlhandled lazgun. The other man was big and wide, speckled with fuzzy freckles. His face wore a broad, unchanging smile.

"We're looking for something," explained the smaller man, his voice thin and chirpy. "I hope to god, for your sake especially, you'll tell us right off where it is."

THE BEAUTIFUL BLONDE android smiled a wide smile out of the small dashboard vidscreen at Gomez. "Good morning, sir," she said in a smooth whispery voice, "and thanks for hitting the Car-Net News button."

"Aren't you informed enough already?" asked Jake, who was piloting their rented skycar through the grey morning sky over Secure Zone 2 of Manhattan.

"Actually it's this platinum *chiquita* who fascinates me," confessed his partner. "Probably due to some genetic defect."

"My name's Marj," continued the synthetic young woman, "and I'm your Menu Guide for the vast array of informative NewsBites—a term fully trademarked by CarNet—available to you this morning. On the international scene there's been a very exciting earthquake in Lisbon—that's in faroff Portugal—and it's estimated to have killed more than 2,500 people. If you want to see the thrilling and heartrending footage, with astute comment by CarNet's respected correspondent Colonel R. W. Estling, request Snippet 1A."

"Give me the domestic menu, *cara.*" Gomez slouched further in his seat.

"Very well, sir." Marj smiled sweetly. "Our top story on the American scene this morning has to do with President Warren Brookmeyer's preparations for his upcoming Cracker Barrel Express Tour of the nation. It is, as you may know, the chief exec's desire to meet face-to-face with as many concerned citizens as it is humanly poss—"

"Hokum," commented Gomez. "How about some cultural stuff?"

"We usually, sir, don't advise anything too deepdish this early in the AM, but I might recommend one of our popular Opinion Essays," suggested Marj. "These in no way reflect the political views or basic beliefs of CarNet News nor of its parent company, MaxComm Communications, nor of its chief exec, Arnold Maxfield, Sr."

"Ay, we can't get away from the case." Gomez slouched further.

"Beg pardon?"

"Thinking aloud."

"We have a brand-new exclusive letter, lasting a full two minutes, in which Professor Joel Freedon discusses his controversial contention that Tek ought to be legalized. He asserts that reports of brain damage, seizures and other serious side effects from this popular illegal electronic drug are purely propaganda circulated by biased and corrupt government agencies. This incisive snippet has the bonus of including some glorious scenery, since it was vidfilmed in the beautiful Carmel Redbout in NorCal only last—"

"Pass," said Gomez.

"We're nearly there," mentioned Jake.

Straightening up, Gomez shut off the newsscreen. "Okay, I'll remain ignorant of the day's major events."

"Dan went through a spell where he thought Freedon was a firstclass guru." Jake tapped out a landing pattern on the dash pad. "Fortunately, he outgrew it."

"Eventually I'll outgrow my fascination with Marj and the news."

Their skycar descended toward a landing port at a Level 18 pedestrian ramp.

Frowning, Gomez leaned forward to look out his side window. "That door that just now came flapping open leads to Richard's floor, doesn't it?"

"Yeah, and that guy who was just tossed out onto the ramp looks like he's one of the operatives assigned to watch him."

6

As the small bald man approached Richard, he steadied his oversized head with his hand, as though he were afraid it might topple completely off his neck. "Forgive us for intruding on your sorrow," he apologized. "But then, in a way, that's why we're here."

"Get the police," Richard told the apartment computer.

"Slow on the uptake," observed the large, freckle-splotched intruder.

"It's the shock of his missus kicking off," said the smaller man. "Dickie—do they call you Dickie or Dick? Doesn't actually matter. Dick, we disabled your security system before we came waltzing in here. Catch?"

"Also your private coppers." His partner laughed in a chesty way.

"What the hell do you want?"

The bald man nodded, which caused his big head to wobble. Steadying it, he replied, "I like that, Dickie, you getting right to the point. We'll get right to business, shall we?" He jabbed at the air with the barrel of his lazgun. "Hand over the vidcaz."

Richard gave a puzzled frown. "The what?"

"Videocassette," amplified the freckled thug.

"The logical assumption, Dick, is that your wife—your late wife—stashed it somewhere in this apartment."

"And the corollary assumption is that you are aware of the location."

"A videocassette?" He shook his head slowly. "We have a few cassettes of parties and such around, plus some of business meetings of Eve's, but—Anyway, none of that stuff is any of your business."

"No, no, Dickie, we're not interested in old memories of bygone days," explained the bald man, gesturing again with his lazgun. "The vidcaz we seek is new, special, made within the—"

"*Pendejos,* play close attention." The vidwall had suddenly returned to life and there stood Gomez, lifesize, smiling amiably out at them. "We've put the whole security system back in service, along with all the other electronic gadgetry you goons futzed up. Cops are winging their way hence even as we chatter. Furthermore, this little diversion of mine has, I'm betting, diverted you to the point that you have completely failed to note the advent of my trusted associate."

"Suppose you dworks raise your hands?" suggested Jake from the doorway behind them.

The bald man started to turn around to face Jake, swinging his lazgun up.

Jake fired the stungun he was holding.

The sizzling beam hit the small man full in the groin. He yowled, went dancing back until he collided with Richard.

Entangled, they both fell over.

The small man's head whapped the floor, bouncing floppily several times.

The other intruder had attempted to tug out his weapon, but a second burst from Jake's stungun knocked him out and into a sprawled position on the sofa.

Walking over, Jake helped Richard up. "I'm Jake Cardigan."

"Yeah, I figured as much," he said. "Your timing was pretty damned good."

Jake asked him, "What about this cassette they're so eager to get hold of?"

"I don't know," he answered. "I don't have any idea what the hell it could be."

◻

THE WHITE-ENAMELED medibot nudged the sprawled body of the little bald man with his metal foot. "Detective or hoodlum?" he inquired of Jake.

Jake was sitting on the arm of the sofa. "The two in here are goons."

"We have to keep them sorted," explained the mechanical man. "Criminals go to a different medical facility." He bent, creaking slightly in the hip joints, to roll the unconscious intruder onto a wheeled stretcher.

As soon as the body hit, the stretcher went rolling across the living room and into the hallway.

Detective Busino came walking in right after the bald man left. "That's the way it goes sometimes, one damn thing after another." He glanced over at Gomez, who was slumped in a tin wingchair. "Hi, Sid. I met you a couple times out in Greater LA when you were still a cop."

"Encounters, Buzz, that have remained fondly etched in my *cabeza.*" Tapping his temple, he came stretching up out of the chair. "I'm with Cosmos now."

"Yeah, I know."

"Yonder is my partner, Jake Cardigan."

Busino studied Jake for a few seconds. "I heard, yeah, that you were out of prison."

"With all charges dropped," reminded Gomez.

"Sure, but they can't give you back the four years you were on ice in the Freezer. Life isn't usually fair." The policeman moved closer to Jake. "Any idea, Cardigan, what's going on?"

"Too soon to tell."

"What brings you to Manhattan?"

"We're looking into Mrs. Bascom's death."

"Not an accident, you think?"

"Too soon to tell."

"I'll be sure to look you up when you finally do have something to tell," promised the officer. "Mr. Bascom, can you add anything?"

"They broke in. I don't know why." Richard was seated stiffly in an armchair, still wearing his outercoat.

Busino crossed to a window. "Always a lot of people coming and going," he observed. "Well, life goes on."

Gomez asked him, "You know either of those louts who busted in?"

"The big one is Chaz Quinlan."

"Let me guess—he's a freelance." Gomez brushed at his curly moustache. "He'll work for just about anybody and he has a lousy memory."

"That's Chaz," agreed Detective Busino. "The other one is Roy Scarbo. Nastier than Chaz and somewhat smarter. He usually does odd jobs for various Teklords in the Tristate area, but he, too, will work for just about anybody who can meet his price."

"It's not likely," observed Jake, "that either one is going to tell us much."

"Nope, they'll end up telling us just about nothing at all." Busino turned to face Richard. "What did they want?"

He shook his head. "They broke in and the bald one—Scarbo? Scarbo pointed a gun at me," he said. "Then Cardigan was here and it was over." He rubbed his hands, slowly, together. "Do you think this has anything to do with my wife's death?"

Busino's smile was small and brief. "I wouldn't," he said, "be at all surprised."

GOMEZ, ON HIS knees in a corner of Eve Bascom's bedroom, was saying, "It's a knack you ought to cultivate, Richard."

"I haven't had much practice." He was sitting, arms hanging at his sides, on his wife's neatly made bed.

"You'll find that being able to lie effectively to the minions of the law is an art that will serve you well throughout life." The detective was running a small handheld sniffer along the floor beside the bed. "No sign of any vidcaz hidden in this part of the room either."

"So you're suggesting that Detective Busino may suspect I wasn't telling him everything I know?"

"Even Little Red Riding Hood would've seen through you."

"You think he suspects I know why those thugs broke in here?"

"He must have an inkling that you were keeping something back, *sí.*"

"Actually, I do some lying in the course of my teaching work. I have to lie to parents now and then, to students, even to my department heads. You'd think, therefore, that—"

"Ah, but lying to civilians is much easier."

A frown suddenly touched Richard's forehead. He jumped up, hurried over to a stack of cassettes they'd already sorted through. "Wait now," he said. "Yes, wait a minute." He grabbed up a vidcaz and held it up.

"Eh?"

"This one was made at a small Larson-Dunn dinner party we had here about a year ago." He approached the wallplayer. "It was a dreadful affair that they pressured Eve into having. For some paroled swindler who was planning to write a faxbook about his colorful career."

Grunting slightly, Gomez rose to his feet and pocketed the sniffer. "You think this is the very cassette those two *pendejos* were seeking?"

"No, but I just now recalled something about this particular gathering." He thrust the caz into the slot. "Show me—what the hell was his name? Larry Seagrove, that's it. Yeah, show me something with Larry Seagrove talking."

"Larry Seagrove," repeated the voxbox of the machine.

"He's on the list," muttered Gomez.

There was a brief humming, a faint clicking. Then a scene blossomed on the wall.

Richard inhaled sharply, then closed his lips tightly together.

His wife was up there on the wall, looking very pretty, standing near a living-room window that looked out on the twilit city.

"Let's see Seagrove," said Richard, anger in his voice.

"Coming up."

A wider shot showed a handsome, though going to fat, man of about forty-five standing beside Eve. He held a glass of dark ale in one hand, his other hand; pudgy tanned fingers, was stroking her bare upper arm. "What's that asshole doing here?" he was asking.

"Larry, love, we're taping this whole evening, remember?"

"So putting this fiasco on tape makes Elroy not an asshole?"

"That's enough." Richard bent his head low, wiping the back of his hand across his mouth.

The image of his wife and the pudgy man faded and the wall was empty.

"I only met Seagrove once." Richard's voice was husky. "But I ought to have recognized that slurred, drunken voice of his."

"He's the *cabrón* who phoned you last night?"

"I'm certain of it," he answered. "Seeing that label on the vidcaz earlier must've triggered my memory. Yes, he's the one who called me."

"This *gordito* works at Larson-Dunn, too, doesn't he?"

Richard stared at him for a few silent seconds. "He does, but how'd you know that?"

Gomez looked away. "We have a list of all the employees. It's an unusual name and it stuck in my *cabeza.*"

"Yes, he worked with Eve here in Manhattan."

Gomez went to the open doorway. "Jake," he called into the living room. "Cease your labors for a moment and get in here, *por favor.*"

"Found something?"

"Not what we were looking for, but interesting none the less."

7

"DAMN IT, I can handle this myself," Richard insisted to Jake.

They were standing in the living room, toe to toe.

"Probably so," conceded Jake. "But you're going to stay home and keep out of it."

"Simply because you work for my father doesn't mean you can order me around like a—"

"Consider this," cut in Jake. "Somebody killed your wife. Then two thugs broke in here to work you over."

"I'm not afraid of getting hurt, if that's what you mean," he said, his voice climbing. "I'm capable of going over to Larry Seagrove's and asking him what the hell he knows."

Jake took two steps back. "Capable of asking him maybe," he said. "But not necessarily capable of getting the right answers. I know what you're feeling, but you're going to have to let us work this case our way."

"To you it's a case, nothing but a job. But *my* wife was murdered," shouted Richard. "I mean to find out why Seagrove phoned me last night."

"Momentito," cut in Gomez, who was sprawled on the bright sofa. "I'd like to suggest that both you *hombres* calm down. You want to find out what happened to your wife and so do we." He planted his feet on the rug and rested his palms on his knees. "Jake and I, however, know more about doing this sort of work. If you mess up, you'll not only lose us valuable information, but you may very well end up defunct." He lifted his hands and

clapped them together once. "This is a purely selfish motive, Ricardo, but I don't want to have to go home to GLA and report to Walt Bascom that I allowed his favorite *hijo* to do something stupid."

"I can see that, yes, but still—"

"The Continental Agency is sending over a fresh batch of operatives," continued Gomez. "Stalwart lads and, I am assured, smarter than the last crew and able to do a crackerjack job of looking after you. Stay here and as soon as we find out anything, you'll be filled in and totally informed."

"It's just that I feel I should do something."

"Anger always gets in the way of an investigation."

Sighing, Richard shrugged and turned away from them. "All-right, okay," he said. "I'll sit it out—for now."

Jake moved to the doorway. "We'll track Seagrove down and talk to the guy."

Gomez said, *"Amigo,* I'm going to leave that chore to you," he announced. "I have a few contacts of my own in this bustling metropolis that I want to drop in on."

THE MIDMORNING SUN warmed the small Level 13 pedramp park. Gomez was sitting on a bench amid the holographic projections of oaks and maples, his portable vidphone resting on his lap.

Something was wrong with the simulated grass surrounding his neowood bench and it kept changing color, flickering from green to blue to purple and then to green again.

"You know what you need, sir?"

"Privacy," answered Gomez.

A heavyset young black man had stopped in front of him. He'd been pushing a wheeled vending cart that had BOOX—CLASSICS WHILE U WAIT! labeled on its side. "Something to read is what you need," he amplified. "My name is Enery."

"Enery, begone."

"How about trying our popular Boox version of *Oliver Twist?*

Specially condensed for modern readers by our expert staff of university-trained experts for your reading pleasure," recited Enery, smiling broadly down at the seated detective. "And here comes the best part—it only takes fourteen minutes to read."

"I can read your entire version of *Oliver Twist* in fourteen minutes?"

"Bright fellow like you might knock it off in eleven," answered the book vendor. "I can see the idea excites you."

"Excitement isn't exactly what your product inspires in me, Enery old man," he said. "But you should've hit me earlier. I already went and read the damn thing in its original form." He made a shooing motion with his right hand.

"Too bad, sir, what a waste of time. Well, then how about taking a crack at *Hamlet?* Reading time seven minutes."

"How about I toss you and your wandering press off the ramp and into oblivion?"

"You're obviously not interested in the lowpriced spread of literature," concluded Enery. "So long, sir." He pushed on.

Gomez pushed out a number on his phone.

A ball-headed robot appeared on the screen. "Secure Zone Two Police Headquarters/Precinct B," it said. "Personal Line 16."

"Sergeant Ramirez, *por favor.*"

"Who's calling?"

"None other than Sid Gomez from out of the West."

"Seashore or mountains?"

"Qué?"

"What sort of scenic footage do you want to watch while you're waiting?"

"Neither."

The screen turned black.

Whistling quietly, Gomez watched the grass fluctuate.

A thickset man popped up on the screen, scowling. "What nerve. Don't you remember, *cholo,* what I told you the last time you attempted to bother me?"

"As I recall, Roberto, you swore undying devotion and—"

"No, not at all, on the contrary, *burrito.* I informed you that I wanted absolutely nothing to do with shady SoCal private eyes."

"Odd, I have no recollection of—"

"You've got to quit intruding on my police work, asking favors," warned the glowering policeman. "It violates all sorts of regulations and, in addition, Sid, it gives me a pain in the butt personally."

"Accept my apologies."

"For as long as you're hanging around our fair city this time, *amigo,* stay the hell away from me," advised Sergeant Ramirez. "Oh, and let me give you one more bit of advice. Shed that gaudy Hollywood Sector jacket you're wearing and buy yourself some conservative Manhattan clothes. *Adiós.*"

He vanished from the phone, replaced by an impressive long shot of the Maine coastline.

Smiling, Gomez slipped the phone in his pocket and stood up.

THE YOUNG WOMAN made another slow, thoughtful circuit of Gomez. "I guess we might, maybe, I don't know, be able to help you," she said dubiously, tugging at a strand of her long dark hair. "The claim of the Park Avenue Haberdashery, afterall, is that we can fit anyone. But in your case . . ." She shrugged with both shoulders and both hands.

The detective said, "I didn't actually come here to be outfitted, *señorita,* so . . . But what exactly is bothering you about me?"

"I'd like to drag one of our servobots in on this." She leaned far to the right, scrutinizing him up and down. "Probably, though I doubt it, our computers can whip up at least a partial solution to your problems."

"What problems? I don't have sartorial problems."

"You're seriously lopsided."

"I don't happen to be lopsided at all," he insisted. "My body is, in fact, so close to perfection that you could use it as a model for heroic statues or—"

"This shoulder," she said, patting the left one, "doesn't match your other one."

"You caught me in the act of shrugging and . . . But wait." He held up his hand in a stop-gesture. "You're sidetracking me. Pay attention now. I want to visit Dressing Room 6 and then try on three pairs of plaid overalls."

"You'll look even stranger in plaid," she assured him. Then she snapped her fingers. "Oh, it's that password nonsense. You're one of Bob's cronies."

"That I am. One of his least lopsided cronies."

"Where'd you get that jacket you're wearing?"

Gomez repeated, "Plaid overalls."

"Oh, right, yes. Come along this way." She guided him through the rows of robot manikins to the rear of the clothing store. "Part of a costume maybe?"

"Eh?"

"Your jacket. Or maybe it's a disguise?"

"This happens to be, *chiquita,* a very stylish piece of wearing apparel," he informed the young woman. "The truth is it's fresh from SoCal and, therefore, at the forefront of fashion. Here in this backwater of society, you haven't as yet—"

"Malarkey," she observed. "Anyhow, here's Dressing Room 6."

He scowled for a few seconds before entering the dressing room. He slid the door shut behind him and then tapped three times on the mirror with his left thumb.

When the mirror moved silently aside, Gomez hopped over into the shadowy room behind it.

Sitting in one of the three straightback chairs was Sergeant Ramirez. "You're in Manhattan about the Eve Bascom murder, aren't you?"

Gomez cocked his head. "So you lawmen are admitting it is murder?"

"Officially the police are admitting just about *nada.*"

"Why is that, *amigo?*"

Ramirez shifted in his chair. "I'm not sure, Sid, exactly what is going on," he answered. "But the lid has been clamped down tight on this one. In fact, when your call came in there was a government agent right outside my cubicle talking, in a very low voice, to Detective Busino and Lieutenant Naprstek. That's why I rerouted you over here to my uncle's place."

Gomez sat. "What kind of government agent, Roberto?"

"This guy didn't identify himself to me and I haven't asked anybody. I'm not, see, officially on this case at all," he told his friend. "I'd tag him Office of Clandestine Operations or some similar sneaky outfit."

Gomez tugged at his moustache and scanned the ceiling. "Why should the OCC be interested in the late *señora?*"

"Got no idea," answered Ramirez. "And, being a few years older than you, I'm no longer interested in solving such puzzlers. I don't care to get messed up in anything that might screw up my retirement plans."

"You set up this meeting, though."

"We're still buddies after all, Sid. And I think I can pass along a tip that might help."

"I'm wondering what sort of tip an *hombre* who knows nothing can give me."

"It could be I know a little something," admitted the police sergeant. "Of course, the absolutely best advice I could give you would be to *vamos* back to SoCal *muy pronto.* But I know you won't pay attention to that."

"*Sí.* I won't."

"We'll move along to Tip #2," said Ramirez. "Go talk to Charley Charla. He's up in Spanish Harlem—right near the White Harlem border—these days. He might know something you want to know."

Gomez frowned. "Charla? He used to specialize in peddling information on Central American and Latin American politics and the Tek trade down that way."

"He still does," said Ramirez.

8

THE FINAL RECEPTIONIST Jake encountered as he penetrated deeper into the Larson-Dunn offices was human. The first had been an ivory-trimmed, silverplated android, the second a handsome suntanned android. The third receptionist was a woman in her late thirties with bright crimson hair and a pale puffy face.

"I'm Jake Cardigan." He leaned and rested his left fist on the far edge of her rubberoid desk.

"Miss McDonnell," said the voxbox in the desktop. "May I introduce Miss McDonnell, Mr. Cardigan."

"Pleased to meet you." He lifted his hand and took a step back. "I'm with the Cosmos Detective Agency and—"

"Oh, I've heard of you." The redhaired woman's voice was dim and somewhat fuzzy.

"I'd like to talk to Larry Seagrove. His apartment tells me he's not at home," explained Jake. "Is he at work today?"

Miss McDonnell furrowed her brow, then glanced over her shoulder. "No, he's not, but . . ." She looked up at a security camera in the distant grey ceiling. "If Larry were in some kind of trouble, could you . . . No, I'm sorry, sir, Mr. Seagrove is out of the office on confidential business. He'll be away for several days."

A door across the large grey reception room had come flapping open. "You, Cardigan." The thin darkhaired woman who'd appeared in the opening beckoned to him. "Get on in here."

"Who might you be, ma'am?" he inquired, not moving.

"I'm Andre Larson. This is my agency." She made an impatient summoning gesture with her right hand. "C'mon, c'mon—I want to see you."

The receptionist gave Jake a fleeting look of sympathy.

Grinning, he entered Andre Larson's office.

"Sit. No, in the black chair." She moved behind her clear Lucite desk.

Settling into the white chair, Jake asked, "Do you know where Larry Seagrove is?"

The high walls of the large, chill room were covered with dozens of small viewscreens. Silent images unfolded on each and every one—newscasts, interviews, documentary footage about a variety of businesses and industries, stock market quotations, animated charts, animated schematic drawings. Andre gestured with her right hand and every screen went blind. She said, "He's out of the office."

"Any specifics? A direction maybe? North? South?"

"Here's exactly what I have to say to you, Cardigan." Her long fingers touched the steel frame of a holophoto of a thickset blonde woman and a thin blonde girl of ten. "I know you're digging into Eve Bascom's death and I want you to understand that Eve, rest her soul, died in an accident."

Jake said, "There's really no way, Miss Larson, that you can know for sure that—"

"*Mrs.* Larson." She tapped the picture. "My wife and daughter."

"Okay, Mrs. Larson, there isn't any way that you, or anyone else at this stage, can know for certain it was an accident."

"The police don't agree with you, Cardigan," she informed him. "They've ruled her death accidental and I accept that. Whatever happened to poor Eve had absolutely nothing to do with any Larson-Dunn client nor with any business activities of this organization. Is that clear to you?"

"Eve's been dead less than twelve hours and you've determined all that already, huh?"

"We've had earlier encounters with Walt Bascom and that

band of grifters he calls a detective agency," she said. "I don't want to see Cosmos spread any further negative stories about my public relations agency."

"What accounts was Eve working on?"

"Her husband can tell you all that." She rose to her feet. "Now, get out, Cardigan."

He remained seated. "Last night who'd she have dinner with?"

"I don't have any further time for you."

He eased up from the chair. "I appreciate this little interlude, ma'am."

"Keep in mind that you're nowhere near as smart as you seem to think you are," she warned. "Remember, too, that I can make a whole hell of a lot of trouble for you."

The office door snapped open. "And I can do the same for you, Mrs. Larson."

Out in the reception room Miss McDonnell said, "You got a vidphone message while you were in there, Mr. Cardigan." She passed him a slip of paper.

It read: *1 PM. Mundy's Pub. Please!*

He pocketed it. "Thanks," he said. "I'll take care of that."

THE ARCADE AT the Level 10 exit to the building that housed the Larson-Dunn offices was thick with roving midday shoppers and seated lunchers. Robot waitresses in bright polkadot aprons were deftly wending their way through the wide circular dining area that was surrounded by small shops.

There were several large animated billboards floating high above the tables. One was extolling the virtues of Mechanix International's servomech division. It showed a chromeplated maidbot efficiently cleaning up a large kitchen, supervising the dinner-fixing equipment and monitoring two pretty blond young children in their nursery. The slogan MI SERVOS—THEY'RE ALMOST HUMAN was superimposed over the doorsized screen at five-second intervals.

Another animated sign depicted a sunbright field of rippling grain. FARMBOY INDUSTRIES—FEEDING AMERICA FROM THE HEART OF FARMLAND flashed across the scene.

Wincing, Jake started for an exit that led to the nearest ped-ramp.

Someone at a small table at the outer rim of the dining circle hailed him. "Cardigan, if you can spare a moment."

Jake made his way over to the table. He recognized the short, thickset man in the dark suit and the robot who was sharing his small table. "Hi, Nate," he said, betraying not a shade of enthusiasm.

The robot started to rise. "You snubbing me, jailbird?"

"Enough, Sunny," warned Nathan Anger.

"He's got no call to highhat me."

Jake grinned at both of them. "Sunny, I mistook you for one of the waitresses," he explained. "Should have noticed you weren't wearing an apron."

"Keep needling me, jocko, and—"

"Quit, Sunny," Anger ordered.

"What brings you up from DC, Nate?"

"Sit for a moment, so we can have a talk."

"Don't really have time."

"Hey, when we tell you to sit, buddy, you damn well better—"

"That's allright," cut in Anger, patting Jake on the sleeve. "You stand if you want. I simply wanted to pass on a cordial warning, Jake."

"From the Office of Clandestine Operations?"

"From friend to friend."

"I don't think we have the right cast to play that scene."

Anger said, "Eve Bascom had an unfortunate accident. I can sympathize with Bascom's son—Richard, is it? I can sympathize with him, and I can even understand that he can't readily accept the fact that it was nothing more than an accident."

"Sure, an accident," said Jake. "Which is why the OCO is warning me off."

Sunny said, "You could have an accident, too, smartass."

"That's enough," cautioned the OCO agent. "This isn't a threat. But it would be, really, much smarter and safer to forget this one."

"I'll think that over, Nate."

"One of the things that concerns us is the way you're bothering Andre Larson," continued Anger. "The Larson-Dunn organization happens to work for certain clients, both here and in Latin America, whose continued peace of mind and wellbeing the government of the United States is interested in. Trouble for L-D might very well lead to trouble for them. None of this has anything to do with the late Mrs. Bascom."

"I'm glad you took the time to set me straight, Nate." Jake gave him a lazy salute. "Don't get rusty, Sunny."

"Wiseass," muttered the robot as Jake left them.

Out on the Level 10 ramp Jake walked for several minutes. When he came to a plump woman who was sitting on a restbench with her purple-tinted poodle, he halted. "Nice boy," he said, patting the animal on the neck.

"It's a *she,*" said the woman, smiling. "Her name is Lulu."

"Hi, Lulu. She must be a great companion to you." He succeeded in transferring the tiny electronic tracking bug that Anger had planted on his sleeve to the dog's fur. "Going to be taking a walk?"

"As soon as I catch my breath."

"A long one?"

"We like to cover about two miles of ramps every day at least."

"Splendid." Jake continued on his way.

9

THE DRIVER OF the skycab said, "This is, absolutely, far as I go, pal."

"We're still three blocks from my destination," Gomez pointed out as the vehicle commenced dropping down through the sky over SemiSecure Zone 3.

The driver told him, "Can't be helped, pal. This café you want happens to be just two short blocks from the White Harlem border—and we never go that close." He tapped the mapscreen on his control panel, where a warning red arrow had commenced flashing over a street grid of the neighborhood.

"Company policy."

"Far be it from me to buck company policy," said the detective. "You *hombres* are, I take it, afraid of the Axis Brotherhood?"

"Cautious, pal, we're cautious." The skycab settled down on a landing lot. "Those Nazi bastards control that whole fifteen-square-block patch over across the border. They are, to a man, a rotten and quarrelsome bunch."

"Do they ever spill over here into Spanish Harlem?"

"Been known to."

Settling his fare, Gomez slid free of the cab. "Thanks for taking me this far," he said as the cab rose upward.

There were no pedramps in this part of the town and the skycar got up and away rapidly.

Sitting on an empty neowood crate next to the narrow entrance to the Café Francisca was a skinny man with a rusty metal right leg showing through his tattered khaki trousers. "I'm a Brazil vet, *señor,*" he informed Gomez. "Can you help out?"

"*Sí.*" After passing him a $5 chit, Gomez inquired, "You know Charley Charla?"

"Might." He slipped the money away into a side pocket.

"Is he about?"

"Who're you?"

"The celebrated, some say fabled, Sid Gomez."

The undernourished man gave an affirmative nod. "Take the first door on your right after you go in. Charley you'll find two levels down."

The hallway of the café smelled richly of spices and cooking oils. Gomez entered the indicated door.

Three steps into the darkness beyond the door a metal hand took hold of his throat. "Where you bound, *gringo?*"

"To consult with Charley," Gomez managed to gasp out. "And, hey, I'm no *gringo.*"

Thin yellowish light blossomed around them. Gomez discovered he was in a greywalled corridor and that a large robot, much dented and long ago painted yellow, had a grip on his neck.

The bot asked, "Who sent you?"

"Bob Ramirez."

"How's old Bobby doing?"

"Well, he's overweight and, frankly, I think the closer he gets to retirement the less nerve he shows." Gomez tapped at the fingers that were still circling his throat. "Can you loosen up, *hermano?*"

"*Sí,* surely." The hand let go and pointed at a green doorway across the way. "Go down the ramp and you'll find Charley's office."

Charla was a small man in a large white suit. In his late fifties, intricately wrinkled and with a moustache that was much fuller and fuzzier than the one the detective sported. "You call that a moustache?" he asked as he nodded at Gomez's upper lip and beckoned him into the small office.

"I used to call it an eyebrow, but that confused people." He sniffed, glancing around the dimlit place. "What's that smell, Charley?"

"Mildew."

"Didn't know mildew could spoil." Gingerly, he sat on the sprung flowered sofa that faced the small folding table the information peddler was using for a desk. "Ramirez suggested I drop in on you."

"He told me." Charla grabbed up an oldfashioned manila folder from a pile on the table. He opened it and set it out in front of him. There was nothing inside. "We'll put your five hundred dollars in here."

"Is this going to be a magical trick?"

"It's my fee, *tonto.*"

"Give me a hint of what I'm buying for this enormous amount of money."

Charla shut the folder, picked it up and fanned himself with it a few times. "I'll give you a sample." When he smiled, dozens of new wrinkles joined the permanent collection on his weathered face. "The killing of Eve Bascom was a collaborative effort."

When Gomez leaned back, the ancient sofa made a loud spong noise. *"Bueno,* Carlito," he said. "That little snippet of news is worth about ten bucks. So you owe me another four hundred and ninety dollars' worth."

"I can't pass on information if you keep butting in with prattle, Sidney," he warned. "The collaboration in question was between a United States government intelligence agency and certain members of the ruling junta in Nicaragua."

"Are we, perhaps, alluding to the Office of Clandestine Operations?"

"That's right, the OCO is into this up to here." He brushed at his wrinkled neck.

"And who down in Nicaragua?"

"I don't have the details yet, Sidney." He dropped the folder, reopened it, pushed it closer to the detective. "Are we going to do some business?"

"Three hundred dollars tops."

"Four hundred and fifty is my bottom price."

"Three fifty."

"Four hundred."

"A deal."

"Part of the funding for this job came from the Nicaraguan embassy in DC," Charla told him. "The pair of *cabróns* in the skyvan that did in the *señora* were recruited right here in Spanish Harlem."

"Hired to commit suicide?"

Charla gave a dry, wheezy laugh. "Doublecrossed, Sidney," he answered. "They thought they were merely going to slam her out of the skylane and then rough her up a little when she landed." He laughed again, drier and wheezier. "What they didn't know—and this certainly teaches us how important it is to keep as well-informed as possible—was that a powerful bomb had been planted in their vehicle, rigged to go off the instant they hit her skycar."

Gomez sat up and the sofa whanged again. "The cops, surely, Charley, would have gathered up some scraps of a bomb."

"Of course they did."

"Were they bribed to keep quiet?"

"No, they were advised to write this up as an accident."

"By who?"

"Somebody in DC."

"The OCC—and anybody else?"

"That's all I have so far."

"How about the name of the *hombre* in the Nicaraguan embassy who helped fund the caper?"

Charla shook his head. "I don't have that as yet, *mi amigo*," he said. "For an additional fee, though, I can continue researching this whole sad affair."

"Do that."

"Another three hundred dollars."

"Two hundred."

"Two fifty."

"Okay." Gomez stroked his moustache. "Now—can you tell me *why* Eve Bascom was knocked off?"

"That I don't have at the moment," he admitted. "I suspect, however, that it must have something to do with the lady's recent sojourn in Managua."

"What about the recent demise of her chum, Arnold Maxfield, Jr., in that selfsame Nicaraguan capital?"

"So far I have nothing on that. Yet I sense there is a link."

Gomez asked, "Anything else you can tell me?"

"Only that you're dealing with some very rough and ruthless people on this one, Sidney. Be careful, *mi amigo.*"

"I intend to." He stood, taking $400 from an inner pocket and tossing it into the yawning folder. "I'll be in touch, Charley."

The informant closed the folder. *"Hasta luego."*

When Gomez emerged up on the street, the panhandling vet was no longer there. Even his crate was gone and the shops in the vicinity were all shut up. There was an uneasy silence hanging over the neighborhood.

He became aware of a rumbling, rattling sound growing in the distance. From around a corner rolled a large landvan. It was painted a brilliant red and in a large white circle on its metal side was emblazoned a large black Nazi swastika. A second landvan, painted exactly like it, came rumbling in its wake.

An amplified voice boomed out, "Looking for trouble, greaser?"

"WHO GETS THE soyloaf grinder?" asked the gunmetal robot waiter.

"The lady," Jake told him.

"Done." The waiter set down the plate. "And you must be having the nomeat meatball sandwich."

"Exactly."

"Enjoy." He went rolling off across the small shadowy dining room.

"My first name is Megan, by the way," said the redhaired Miss McDonnell in her small voice. They were sitting in a booth at the back of Munsey's Pub. There were less than thirty people in the booths and at the scattering of tables. Over near the bar two men in grey business suits were playing vidwall darts. "The food isn't especially good, but nobody from the office ever comes here. That makes it a fairly safe location to talk, Mr. Cardigan."

"And you have something to talk about, Megan?"

She lowered her voice. "About the man you're looking for."

"Do you know where I can find the guy?"

"First I need to know exactly why you're hunting for him."

Jake said, "Has to do with Eve Bascom's death. I think maybe he's got some information about that."

She slumped, hands dropping into her lap. "I was afraid that's what this was about," she told him forlornly. "She's going to keep hurting him even after she's dead."

"I know he was involved with her at one time."

"Yes, he was." Her voice rose, grew louder. "That whore."

Jake rested an elbow on the tabletop. "What about you and Seagrove?"

"We're friends," she said. "Before he got embroiled with her, we were closer."

"He wasn't still seeing her, was he?"

"Not, no, in the way he used to, not since she took to fooling around with young Maxfield," answered Megan. "But she still took advantage of him, had him running errands, doing favors. I know she's dead, but she was a dreadful bitch."

"Any idea who killed her?"

"The vidnews said it was an accident . . . but it wasn't, was it?"

"Don't think so."

"Then he could be in danger, too."

"He must think he is, if he's gone into hiding."

"You—and your detective agency—you're in a position to see that nothing bad happens to him."

"We can protect him, yeah," he assured her. "Unless he's directly tied in to her murder."

"No, he's an innocent bystander. Well, innocent in the sense that he had nothing to do with her death."

Jake asked, "Where's he hiding?"

"When . . ." She began very quietly to cry. "Whenever he's in trouble, he turns to me."

"I can help him get out of it," he said. "Tell me where he is."

"Connecticut." Her voice fell to a whisper. "In a town called Southport." She gave him an address. "It's a waterside house that belongs to my uncle."

"Is Seagrove there alone?"

"Yes, entirely. My uncle's out in NorCal on an extended business trip."

"Can you contact Seagrove?"

She nodded.

"Okay, then call him—make sure you use a tapproof phone—and let him know I'll be out there this afternoon to talk with him," Jake instructed. "After I see him, I'll arrange to have him stashed someplace safe until this mess gets resolved."

"This mess, as you call it," she said, "may never get entirely resolved, Mr. Cardigan. It is, I suspect, an *enormous* mess."

"Meaning?"

"That's all I can say."

THE PRESIDENT OF the United States was pacing his large private office several levels below the White House. A tall, slender black man in his middle fifties, he was keeping his eyes on the small holostage in the corner. "I've been thinking, Tony, that, probably, I don't have to do this at all."

The figure projected on the stage wore an offwhite medical jacket. "I wish, Mr. President, you'd address me as Anthony. The name Tony has never—"

"All right, Anthony. What I'm trying to get at, Doctor, is that I don't, I'm just about convinced, have to go through with—"

"It's absolutely essential that you do something, and very

soon," interrupted Dr. Marchitelli. "Now, we've been over all this in previous interviews. Everything has been agreed on, the whole operational plan is in place. You'll be checking into the clinic in a very few days now."

"Yes, but I owe it to the American people to remain on the job."

"You can't do anything like a competent job while you're addicted."

"Addiction is a strong word, Tony, a very strong word," said President Brookmeyer. "Mild habituation is more the—"

"You're completely *hooked* on Tek. All the tests confirm that, as does your previous testimony to me," the doctor told him, impatience sounding in his voice. "When you finish your stay with us, you'll be able to avoid Tek."

"I had a long chat with Vice President McCracklin last evening, Doctor, and he agrees that perhaps we went overboard in—"

"I talked to him less than an hour ago. He agrees that you must come down here, Mr. President."

"He must have changed his mind again."

"Getting you into the facility secretly is, as you're already aware, a very tricky business," reminded Dr. Marchitelli. "As of now everything is set for your coming. If we abort the operation now, it might well cause leaks to the media and make it impossible for you to come sometime later."

"Yes, yes, I'm aware of that," conceded the president. "It's the secret, sneaky you might call it, nature of all this that upsets me, Tony—Anthony. I believe the American people would be greatly disappointed were they to learn I did something like this."

"They'll be more upset if they find out for certain that the rumors about your flirting with Tek are all true," the doctor said evenly from the pedestal. "You have to get rid of your addiction and you have to do it right away."

Brookmeyer sighed. "My wife agrees with you," he said quietly. "Very well, I'll go ahead with this."

"It's for the best," said the image of the doctor.

10

THE FIRST AXIS Brotherhood van shuddered to a stop in front of the Café Francisca. A side door, which carried a large swastika painted on it, rattled open and young men in black neoleather uniforms came doubletiming out onto the street. Each wore a crimson helmet with a double eagle engraved on it in silver and each carried a long black stunrod.

Gomez had by this time withdrawn to the other side of the street and was heading away from the arriving Axis Brotherhood raiders.

Now a large, thick young man jumped down from the driveset. "Hey, greaser! I'm not through talking to you," he shouted after Gomez. Across his broad, blackclad chest he held a lazrifle.

Ignoring him, Gomez increased his pace.

The second crimson van had rattled to a stop behind the first. From out of it a dozen more uniformed youths were pouring. Instead of stunrods, they carried bullhorns and leaflets.

The husky young man who was interested in the departing Gomez doubled back, snatching a bullhorn from one of the other uniformed youths. "There goes an ethnik who's defying us," he announced over the bullhorn. "Let's teach him!"

Gomez spun around, yanked out his stungun and fired.

The sizzling beam slapped the young man with the bullhorn smack in the chest. He gave an awking yell that was amplified and went echoing up and down the narrow street. Then he took three wobbly steps to his right and fell over in the gutter.

Gomez concentrated on running.

"Get the spick!" someone shouted.

"Stop that greaser!"

"Doesn't sound," Gomez told himself as he sped along, "like a time for peaceful negotiations."

"Bring him down!"

"Stun the bastard!"

"Lazgun him!"

Running ever faster, Gomez went skidding around the corner.

As he passed the doorway of a fortune-telling shop, the door snapped suddenly open and blocked his progress. A huge metal arm came snaking out, a hand grabbed his arm and yanked him inside.

Larry Seagrove, sniffling, pointed at the sprawled butler with a right hand that quivered slightly. "Sure, you can do something, can't you, Cardigan?" He grabbed his right hand with his left and pressed it to his chest.

"What happened to him?"

They were standing in the middle of the large living room of the Southport home where Seagrove was hiding out. All the windows had been blanked and the vidwall was dark. Stretched out, facedown, in the middle of the brightlit room was a darksuited android.

"He fell over," explained Seagrove, letting go his right hand so he could wipe at his nose. "He hit his damn head." He walked over toward an unseeing window. "It's an expensive andy, one of the topline Mechanix International models. I couldn't afford one myself. But Megan's damned uncle, he'll piss and moan about it. He'll blame me."

Jake poked the fallen android with his boot toe. "What'd you hit him with?"

"I didn't touch him, didn't lay a hand on him," he insisted, sniffling. "Jesus, Cardigan, whose side are you on here? I'm helping you out, remember? You've no right to go accusing me of busting up the old bastard's servos."

"Somebody took a blunt instrument to the butler's skull," said Jake evenly. "He didn't get that bunged up just falling. You have an argument with him?"

"No, not exactly. But, hell, Cardigan, he was a snotty son of a bitch. You know, they build them that way. Program the bastards to act like you weren't worth shit. I have permission, afterall, to stay here."

"You can have a repair squad come look at him after we take care of our business."

"Why the hell should I do that? I don't want to get stuck with the bill for the work, which is why I was hoping you could give me a hand patching him up." Seagrove sniffled. "Here in Connecticut they think you're a millionaire if you live in Southport. A repair bill that would cost five thousand dollars in Manhattan will run you fifteen thousand around here. Besides, he's a servo, which means he was supposed to serve me and not go around insulting me all the damn time. The way I—"

"We can settle the butler matter later, Seagrove." Stepping over the battered android, Jake approached the man. "Before I get you moved to a safer hideaway, I—"

"This place was safe," he said. "If Megan hadn't shot off her mouth to you, nobody would know where I was."

"Maybe."

"What do you mean?"

"Figure it out," suggested Jake. "I found you. Others can."

"Others—what others, for Christ sake?"

"The others who killed Eve. The others who broke in on her husband, looking for the vidcaz."

Seagrove wiped at his nose. "They don't know I have the damn cassette, do they? Megan doesn't know, so I don't see how they—"

"Look, I'm not sure yet of all that's going on," cut in Jake. "But I do know we're dealing with folks who'll kill to get what they want. And apparently they'd like to have the cassette."

"Okay, allright," he said. "Suppose I hand it over to you? That should stop them from hunting for me. That sounds right, doesn't it? It makes sense."

"Some sense, yeah. What's on the cassette?"

Seagrove shook his head. "I don't know," he swore. "I have, you know, a general idea, but honest to god, Cardigan, I never actually looked at the cassette itself, never played it. Never, not once. That way nobody can say, 'That asshole Seagrove knows what she knew, let's ice him, too.' "

"Eve gave you the vidcaz?"

"Yes, right. The day she found out that Junior—Arnie Maxfield, Jr., that toad—that he was dead. That night she stopped by, said she'd put a message on tape. It was important and I was to keep it for her."

"In what way important?"

"Okay, this is all, really, I know," began Seagrove. "Eve was down in Managua on Larson-Dunn business. The manager of the Mechanix International operation in Nicaragua was in some sort of mess and, since we have the MI public relations account down there, she was assigned to make him look like less of a crook than he is." He paused to fish out a handkerchief. "I've had this damn cold for a week. Can't seem to shake it."

"What happened in Nicaragua?"

"It had, far as I can tell, nothing to do with the client." He blew his nose, then balled up the handkerchief in his hand. "Arnie, though, was down there on some business or other for his father—that's MaxComm, you know—and he found out something. After he was killed, Eve got very upset and she told me it wasn't an accident. She was certain someone had killed him."

"What had he found out?"

"I'm not sure, but it was sure as hell something he wasn't supposed to know."

"Did Eve tell you who she suspected had killed Maxfield?"

"No, but she was afraid they were going to come after her."

"Which means he'd shared what he knew with her."

"Exactly. That's why she was so scared."

Jake asked, "Why couldn't she go to the police?"

"She didn't want to risk that," said Seagrove, sniffing. "My feeling is, you know, that Eve wasn't too sure who she could trust. She put what she knew on the vidcaz and she told me, if anything happened to her, to give the thing to her husband."

"She probably told somebody else about the cassette, told them that it existed."

"As insurance, but that didn't work." Seagrove blew his nose. "She told me her husband would know what to do. His old man is—but, hell, you know that since you work for the old bastard."

Jake took a step back. "But you didn't do what she asked you. You didn't hand it over to her husband."

"I decided to look after my own ass, Cardigan. Lie low for a while."

"You phoned him, though."

"I was drunk," he explained. "Well, I'm drunk quite a lot these days. I wasn't going to risk passing the thing to him or even trying to send it. But I thought, you know, I ought to at least give the poor guy a hint. Let him know it was bullshit about her being in an accident."

"How'd you know Eve was dead before her husband did?"

"What?"

"You phoned Richard, told him she'd been murdered," said Jake. "That was before the police had contacted him to tell him about the accident."

"That's because I heard it on the vidnews," Seagrove told him, sniffling. "Listen, Cardigan, I'm not that big a shitcase. If I'd known in advance that they were going to kill her, I'd have gotten her a warning somehow."

"I'll take your word."

"I loved her," he said quietly. "More than that anemic husband of hers, more than Arnie—more than any of them. The trouble is, she quit loving me."

"Where's the cassette?"

"Here. Up in the bedroom I'm using," answered Seagrove.

"Let's," suggested Jake, "go get it."

11

□

THE LARGE COPPERY robot was wearing a star-dotted robe and a turban of similar material. He shut the door, activated the electronic safety barrier and shook his head at Gomez. "Why'd you rile those lunkheads?"

The detective found himself in a small reception parlor. A computer terminal, decorated with the signs of the zodiac, sat on a small round table in the center of the room and there were four straightback chairs lined up against the lefthand wall. At the back of the room velvety black drapes masked a doorway.

Outside in the street he could hear the Axis Brotherhood troopers go stomping by, shouting threats. They'd apparently lost his trail.

"Something about my impressive Latino heritage seems to have set them off," he explained to the robot. "Outside of that, and shooting one of them down, I really didn't do anything to annoy the lads."

"The Street Commandos will take care of them."

"Street Commandos?"

"That's a local group dedicated to keeping them on their side of the border."

"Do people get killed during these skirmishes?"

"Sometimes a few."

The drapes parted to admit a thin young woman of about eighteen. She, too, wore a black robe. "You don't seem to be, if you'll excuse my pointing this out, very bright," she observed.

"The sensible thing to do when these rowdies make one of their propaganda raids is to get the heck off the street. Shooting them willy-nilly, to my way of thinking, isn't the best course of action at all."

"I only felled one." He held up a forefinger. "Who are you, by the way, and why did you haul me in here?"

"I'm Princess Carmelita, the wellknown mystic and fortune-teller," the girl answered. "This is Professor Zingaro, my business associate."

"Did the stars foretell I'd come racing by your doorstep in need of help, Princess?"

"I have a monitoring system that's extremely effective, Señor Gomez."

His eyebrows rose. "Ah, you know me, huh?"

"I learned you'd be dropping in on that old rascal, Charley Charla, and I got curious," she said. "I've heard about you before, that you were an exceptional detective and something of a womanizer." Her small nose wrinkled and she gave a quick dismissive shrug. "You're nowhere near as impressive as your reputation led me to expect."

"Well, my appeal is to more mature minds, *cara,*" he informed her. "Tots, suckling babies and those with the brain capacity of an onion, don't cotton to me as well as do—"

"You're also hotheaded and impetuous. You shouldn't have stungunned Otto out in—"

"Palavering with goons carrying lazrifles, Princess, and calling me names isn't too bright."

She smiled at the big robot. "What did I tell you, Professor?"

"Yep, you were right."

"I appreciate your saving me from the pursuing hordes," said Gomez with a smile. "Now—is there any way to get clear of your establishment without going back onto the street?"

"There's an intelligent remark for a change," said Princess Carmelita. "Follow me, Gomez."

She led him through the draped doorway, along a dimlit hall and up to an unpainted neowood door.

"Take this tunnel to its end—about a mile from here—and you'll come to another door. That'll put you on the street in a safe area."

"Gracias." He put his hand on the doorknob. "Why do you folks put up with these Axis Brotherhood raids?"

"We don't. That is, as a community we don't," she said. "The Street Commandos take care of them when they stray over into Spanish Harlem and there's a similar, very efficient group, over in African Harlem."

"Too many fragments," he commented. "What you need to do is—"

"Let me give *you* a piece of advice." She put her hand against his back and gave him a gentle shove into the tunnel. "Don't trust Charley Charla completely."

Gomez laughed. "Princess, I don't trust anybody completely." He started, carefully, away from her.

ALTHOUGH THEIR HOTEL was in the safe half of Central Park, it gave a view of the unsecured, wild half. From the windows of the tower suite Gomez and Jake were sharing, you could see down across the overgrown parklands, the tangles of trees and brush. Far off on the West Side a portion of the forest was on fire. Grey smoke was pouring up into the coming dusk.

"Ain't nature grand?" remarked Gomez as Jake returned home.

"I tracked down Larry Seagrove." He took the videocassette from his pocket, hefted it on his palm. "He had the caz."

"What did he have to say?"

"Not that much." He told his partner what he'd learned out in Connecticut.

"He doesn't sound like a very admirable *hombre*," observed Gomez when Jake had finished. "You'd think if Eve was going to fool around, she'd have picked somebody who's an improvement on her hubby. Trade up, is my motto."

"Let's watch this." Crossing to the vidwall, Jake slid the vidcaz into the slot.

Eve Bascom appeared on the screen. She was dressed in a simple tan slaxsuit and was sitting in a straight metal chair in the living room of their apartment. Her face was pale, shadows underscored her eyes and her cheekbones.

"She looks," said Gomez, "like she knows she's going to die."

Eve coughed into her hand, then lowered her head for a few seconds. Straightening up, she took a deep breath and looked directly into the camera. "What I'm going to say must be important," she began, running her tongue over her upper lip. "Arnie said it was and . . . I think that's why they killed him. He didn't, Christ, really tell me all he knew. But I'm afraid it's enough . . . enough probably to get me killed. There's something going on . . . something important. It involves the Nicaraguan government, including General Alcazar and the junta, and the American embassy down there is mixed up in this, too. Arnie didn't go into all that . . . I'm talking about Arnold Maxfield, Jr. I guess I ought to get his whole name into this. I forget, Richard, if you even knew that I knew Arnie." She coughed again, held both hands up over her mouth for several seconds. "You'd think, being in the line of work I'm in, that I'd be able to keep all these lies straight. Anyway, some of the big Tek cartels—particularly the Joaquim Cartel, which operates in Nicaragua and Florida—are involved as well. Something is going to happen . . . maybe part of it has already happened. Arnie was cagey about the details. You'd have to know him to understand what I mean." She took another deep breath, exhaled in a sighing way, took in another breath. "Allright, it all centers around something called Surrogate 13. 'That's what they call it, babe,' he told me. 'Surrogate 13. Knowing about that is going to make me very . . . well, you'll see.' He wasn't exactly the smartest or most diplomatic man in the world. Nowhere near as clever as his father. I think that when he tried to parlay what he'd found out . . . well, things went wrong for him." She leaned back in the chair, briefly closed her eyes. "Surrogate 13. It doesn't seem fair, really, to get killed over something I know so little about. Richard, if you ever see this . . . I'm sorry. I really do love you, but . . . but everything just . . ." She gave a faint, sad shrug.

The wall went blank.

12

◻

BASCOM LOOKED TWICE as rumpled as he had the last time they saw him. And nearly all the clutter had returned to his desktop. His saxophone was there, too, sprawled across stacks of memodiscs.

"Surrogate 13," he repeated, shaking his head slowly. "Nope, that means not a damn thing to me." His image, up from lifesize, nearly filled the vidwall of their living room.

Gomez was perched now in the window seat, watching the skywagons trying to control the park fire far to the west. "A substitute for something," he suggested. "A stand-in."

"The thirteenth substitute," said the agency chief. "Or it could just as easily be a substitute for a drug, a product . . . Hell, just about any damn thing."

Jake was straddling a straight chair. "How about an android?"

"Another possibility," conceded Bascom out in his Cosmos Detective Agency office. "Is that just a hunch?"

"Eve was down there in Managua trying to smooth out a mess involving the guy who runs the Nicaraguan office of Mechanix International," Jake said. "Mechanix makes andies."

"Follow up on that," said the chief.

Gomez said, "Before we venture into Central America, *jefe,* I think we better make a stopover in our nation's capital."

"From what you've reported, I agree," said Bascom. "Find out who in the Nicaraguan Embassy hired those thugs to smash into Eve's skycar. I'd like something nasty to befall that lad."

"He's just a cog," said Jake.

"I'm aware of that, but I want the bastard smashed all the same," said Bascom. "This thing, however, is shaping up as something bigger than just a oneshot murder tricked up to seem an accident." He rubbed his fingertips together. "I want to bring down everybody and anybody who had anything to do with killing my son's wife. But if we can uncork an international conspiracy—well, that can be damned lucrative. In terms of both fees and favors and rewards."

Gomez said, *"Chihuahua,* it's the old original chief emerging. I was starting to fear that warm familial feelings had overcome his crass innerself for good."

"You knew that couldn't last," said Jake.

"Enough, you two," warned Bascom. "My main concern is still my son. But I want you to follow this wherever it leads."

"Might be a good idea to talk to someone at MaxComm," suggested Jake. "To get more information on what Maxfield, Jr., was up to down there. Their headquarters office is in New Baltimore, just outside of DC. Do you have any contacts there?"

"I'll check and provide you a name when you get to Washington," the agency head promised. "The OCO is in this, too, huh?"

"As I mentioned, Nate Anger and his pet robot warned me off. A sure sign that they're hooked in somehow."

"You have anyone in the OCO you can tap?"

Jake thought about it. "One possible contact—maybe."

"Use it if you can."

Gomez said, "We'd best tread lightly on this, *amigos.* We're going to be waltzing around with intelligence boys, cutthroat tycoons and probably even Teklords."

Jake stood up, rested his hand on the back of his chair. "What about Eve's message to your son?" asked Jake.

"Eventually he'll have to see it," said Bascom. "But not right yet. Wait until this is all over."

"He may not," said Jake, "be ready for the truth even then."

□

MOST EVENINGS AT this hour Frank Dockert could be found at his club in New Baltimore. Alone, a large black man in his middle forties, he was down on the shooting floor six levels underground. He'd chosen a simulated jungle area tonight and was moving carefully through a stretch of simulated steamy tropical forest, carrying a lazrifle.

He became aware of the spoor of a tiger just seconds before his vidphone buzzed.

Up ahead the dense green foliage flickered as the unseen tiger headed for elsewhere.

"What?" said Dockert.

"Access B2," spoke the phone as he lifted it free of his jacket pocket.

"Go ahead." He sat on a real log that had been placed among the hologram trees and vines.

"I'm sorry to break in on your—"

"Reach a point, Nathan."

Anger said, "We have to assume that Cardigan and Gomez have the vidcaz."

"Why?"

"Because they're leaving Manhattan early tomorrow morning."

"Heading for where, Nathan?"

"They're coming your way, Frank."

"Specifically to me?"

"No, no. They're booked into the Beltway Plaza in DC. They don't know anything about you."

THE PRESIDENT OF the United States sat stiff and straight in the midcabin seat of the military skyvan. "I'm still not convinced we'll get away with this, Jim," he said quietly.

Vice President McCracklin was lean and blond, almost handsome, a few years younger than the president. "We've got the most efficient people possible working with us on this, Warren. Relax, will you."

"A great many things, numerous unforeseen things, can go wrong."

"No, not with something as carefully worked out as this."

The windows were all blanked and they could see nothing of the night sky they were flying through.

"Someone may well find out I'm at the clinic when I'm supposed to be on the tour."

"Not a chance."

"Besides, Jim, I keep telling you and this Dr. Marchitelli that I'm not actually a confirmed Tek addict. True, I admit, I get a lift from using Tek now and then. But, hell, there can't be more than a dozen people in the world who have to deal with as much pressure and stress as I do. So a little Tek session now and—"

"It's a lot more serious than that, Warren. We all know that."

Sighing out a breath, Brookmeyer said, "The other factor that worries me is this damned—stand-in. That's not going to fool anybody or—"

"Mechanix International turns out a very good product. Don't worry."

"I don't know," said the president. "Now that we're actually going ahead with this—I feel extremely uneasy."

"Relax," urged the vice president, smiling. "Everything is going to go exactly as intended."

13

JAKE WAS HEADING his skycar, as per instructions, for a landing at Visitors Lot 3A at the vast MaxComm Communications Centre in New Baltimore.

"Jake Cardigan?" said the voxbox on his control panel.

"Yeah?"

"Whom are you visiting at MaxComm this morning?"

"Already told you—Arlen Sulman, who's with the KwikNews Division." That was the contact name Bascom had provided him with earlier this morning.

"Just confirming, sir."

"Okay."

"You're being rerouted to Personnel Lot 4B," the voice informed him.

"Oh, so?"

"That's on the harborside of Wing 3."

Jake tapped out a revised landing pattern.

His skycar continued dropping down, sailing over the multi-domed central headquarters of Arnold Maxfield, Sr.'s communications empire.

"Jake Cardigan?"

"Right here."

"Further landing revisions, sir," said the MaxComm reception voice.

"Okay, I'm standing by."

"You're to set down in Public Parking Lot 16, which you'll

find directly across the street from the backside of Wing 3. You are not to enter MaxComm property."

"Why is that?"

"After you land at Lot 16, Mr. Sulman will be brought to you."

"Brought?"

"It seems he's having some trouble walking."

THE SMALL, SWEETSMELLING little restaurant was on a short sidestreet just off Nixon Boulevard. When Gomez stepped out of the humid DC morning and into the frilly beflowered dining parlor, he sneezed.

"A nice cup of cranberry tea is just what you need, young feller." A grandmotherly android came up and took hold of his elbow. "Welcome to Granny Gurton's Breakfast Nook. All by our lonesome this lovely morning, are we?"

"No, *gramacita,* we're meeting that gent seated over yonder."

"Tsk," remarked the android. "He's been awfully restless. He really ought to relax more. My sakes, even in a worrier's town like DC he's a standout. Always checking all those watches and—"

"I'll find my way over to him." Extricating himself from the greyhaired android's grasp, Gomez crossed to the table where the young Chinese cyborg was waiting.

"Geez Louise, Gomez," the young man said, rolling up the sleeve on his metal arm. "When we agree to meet at ten-fifteen AM, does that mean ten-seventeen to you?"

"Landsakes, Timecheck, you're turning into a real worrywart." Gomez took the chair opposite him. "What's that on your plate, by the way?"

"Jamcakes with honeyberry sauce. Want an order?"

"No, absolutely not."

"Just look at that." Timecheck tapped the face of one of the many watches built into his metal right arm. "Buenos Aires time is running four seconds off again. I tell you, daddy, the craftsmen these days—"

"Can we rush through all this temporal chitchat and get to the business of the day?"

"Precisely why I'm here, kiddo."

"When I learned that you'd relocated in this citadel of democracy, Timecheck, I figured I'd tackle you first for the information I seek," Gomez told the informant. "Since I've dealt with you fruitfully in various climes and locales."

"I got to tell you that Washington beats them all." Timecheck lifted up a forkful of jamcake. "You recall how glum I was in Japan? Wow, all those Zen types with no idea of deadlines and the swift passage of time. Paris was a terrific improvement. I meant to tell you, daddy, a whole city stuffed with clockwatchers." He took another bite, savoring it. "Ah, but Washington, DC. It's the timebound center of the universe. A microsecond means something in this burg." He pointed his fork ceilingward. "I love it here and inside info abounds, you bump into secrets and scuttlebutt at every turning and—"

"Here's that tea, darling." The Granny android put a teacup in front of Gomez. "Drink that down and just see if that nasty old cold doesn't go right away."

"Gracias."

Timecheck inched his chair back. "You sick?"

"No."

"I don't like to catch colds. For some reason whenever I'm down with one all my clocks run slow."

"I'm in the pink," the detective assured his information source. "Now tell me what you've come up with for me since we spoke on the vidphone an hour ago."

"One hour sixteen minutes ago," corrected Timecheck after consulting two of his builtin watches.

"What have you learned about the activities of the Nicaraguan Embassy?"

Timecheck tapped Gomez's teacup with a metal fingertip. "You planning to drink that?"

"Not in the least."

After appropriating the cranberry tea and enjoying a long sip, Timecheck said, "Not sweet enough."

"Facts," urged Gomez.

"The day before Eve Bascom died, an official at the embassy—one Raoul Martinez—had a visitor," the Chinese told him. "This visitor was Dr. Izabel Morgana, who teaches at the Federal University in Managua. Poli Sci is the lady's subject and, it goes without saying, she has the complete approval of General Alcazar and the junta."

"How does she fit in?"

"After visiting Martinez, she dropped into a sleazy—make that sleazier—section of town to meet with a gent who's been known to help arrange killings for hire up in Manhattan. I can provide his name and background if—"

"Not just yet," said Gomez. "It sounds like Dr. Morgana is somebody I ought to look up."

"To do that, you got to wend your way to Managua," Timecheck told him. "She headed for home at just about the exact moment Eve Bascom was going on to glory."

Gomez said, "Anything on why they—"

"Goodness sake, how're you going to shake that cold if you give your nice tea away, young man?" The android placed another steaming cup in front of Gomez. "Now drink that all down like a good boy."

"Soon as it cools," he promised. "Now shoo."

Timecheck said, "If you were going to inquire into motive, save your breath."

"Nothing?"

"Not so far. All I know is that Dr. Morgana wanted to make absolutely certain that Eve Bascom ceased to be."

"Seems likely she's in cahoots with somebody in the Nicaraguan government."

"Very likely, sure."

Absently Gomez drank some of his cranberry tea. "Keep nosing around," he told the information dealer. "I'll be in touch again soon."

Timecheck eyed him as he stood up. "You certain you haven't got something contagious?"

ARLEN SULMAN WAS a slight, greyhaired man. He was standing near the entrance to Lot 16, being supported by a bored-looking chromeplated robot. Piled up next to him on the paving were three plasticartons, a filebox chockfull of memodiscs and a bundle of faxpapers tied up with real twine.

"But I didn't fall," he was saying to the robot as Jake came walking up to him. "You shoved me."

"I never shoved you," argued the robot. "I was simply helping you along."

"You gave me the old heavho."

"When you're terminated from MaxComm, you have to leave," said the robot. "You don't dawdle, you don't tarry."

"I couldn't very well dawdle with you there throwing me down a ramp."

"It was a nudge, a friendly nudge." The mechanical man noticed Jake. "I'd appreciate it, sir, if you'd help Mr. Sulman hobble to his skybus stop up at the corner. We're not supposed to stray even this far from the MaxComm grounds, but since he claims he has a twisted ankle, I—"

"It's sprained. You can see that."

"I'll help out." Jake took hold of Sulman's arm as the silvery robot stepped clear of him.

"Good luck in your next job, Mr. Sulman," called the robot as it went hurrying away.

"I'm Jake Cardigan."

"Oh, great. Because of you, I'm out on my ear."

"How's that?"

"Well, that has to be the reason. Somebody got wind that I was going to blab to you and—"

"Why would that matter?"

"Because they know you're investigating Eve Bascom's death."

"Does MaxComm have something to hide?"

"They've already got a detective agency of their own looking into Arnie Maxfield, Jr.'s death," explained Sulman. "Since those two cases are likely to link up, I imagine they don't want you gumming up the works."

"What agency is handling the case for them?"

"I don't think I better talk to you. If you'll help me get to the corner, I'll—"

"Which agency?"

"An outfit from out your way. Bev Kendricks & Associates."

Jake grinned. "That's interesting."

"Not to me, Cardigan. What's interesting to me is that shortly after promising to do a favor for Walt Bascom—who, come to think of it, hasn't done a darned thing for me in ages—I get bounced."

"That can't be the only reason."

"Well, there have been some remarks about my getting too old for the news business."

"What's your age?"

"Nearly fifty."

"That's not old."

"Can you help me to that bus stop? I'm afraid I'll fall over if I try to walk on this ankle."

"Okay, lean on me and let's start."

"Wait, my stuff," remembered Sulman. "You'll have to tote that, too."

"Look, I'll prop you up on these cartons, go over and get my skycar and give you a ride home."

"No, I don't want to be seen flying around with you."

"What else can happen?"

"Right now I'm only unemployed. Blacklisted I don't need."

Jake suggested, "You may as well tell me what you know."

"Not a blasted thing do I know, Cardigan."

"You knew that Maxfield, Jr. was involved with Eve Bascom."

"Lots of people around here knew that."

"Do you have any idea why he was killed?"

"I think I'll just abandon this crap here," said Sulman. "I'll make it to the stop on my own."

"Is there anybody else at MaxComm who I can—"

"Nobody."

Jake said, "Suppose I contact Maxfield, Sr., and mention that I had a two-hour chat with you, wherein you passed along all sorts of Maxfield secrets?"

"That would screw me up a lot."

"So give me something useful now."

Sulman told him, "Talk to Karla Maxfield."

"That's Maxfield's daughter?"

"Yes, and she was down in Nicaragua for a few days, too." He glanced across at the huge MaxComm complex. "She's putting in an appearance at a fundraising cocktail party at the War Museum in DC tonight. If you can get into that, you might be able to approach her."

"Okay, let me help you to that skybus stop," offered Jake.

"Forget it," said Sulman. "Today I think I'll splurge and take a cab."

14

GOMEZ WAS STRETCHED out, facedown, on the parlor carpet when Jake returned to their suite at the Beltway Plaza.

"Fatigued, are you?" Jake asked his prone partner.

"Note the dornicks spread out on the coffee table, *amigo,*" grunted Gomez. His investigation of this stretch of carpeting concluded, he got to his knees and dropped the sniffer gadget away in a pocket.

"Three very small bugging devices."

"Makes a fellow feel as though he's infested with ticks or *cucarachas.*" He rose up completely, rubbed at his left buttock and sighed. "I also had to ditch a pretty but inept *señorita* who was doing a secondrate job of trying to tag me. Cute and I was tempted to lure her into a bistro for a friendly ale—but who can dally with a lass who can't even tail somebody without tipping her hand?"

"Yeah, I was trailed for a while, too." Bending, he poked a forefinger at the eavesdropping devices Gomez had collected in their suite. "Swiss manufacture. The type favored by the OCO."

"We already knew they were interested in us." Gomez wandered over to a window. The day was fading away to dusk. "I'd like to know, though, exactly how these Clandestine *cabróns* are connected with all this."

"That's going to take a mite longer to find out than I anticipated," Jake told him. "My contact there is—apparently—out of the country and unreachable. I tried to track him down this afternoon with absolutely no luck." He rested on the arm of the sofa.

"Before we compare notes, there's a vidphone message for you," said his partner, nodding in the direction of the vidwall. "I might mention that, since all these bugs were bugging away when the message came in, the OCO also knows all about your secret love life."

"Huh?"

"Replay the last message, *por favor,*" Gomez instructed the wall.

Alicia Bower's image materialized on the screen. She was wearing a pale green tunicdress and her auburn hair was tied back with a twist of dark green ribbon. She was standing in what looked to be a public vidphone booth at a skyport. "Jake, it's very important that I talk to you," she said, concern sounding in her voice. "I've just found out something and I think it may tie in with the case you're working on. I'm going to be in DC on business today. Meet me at my rooms at the Jefferson Hotel tonight at seven. Please."

As the image faded, Gomez asked, "Think she actually knows something?"

"I'd better go over there and find out." From his jacket pocket he took a small plasticard. "Which means you'll have to attend these festivities alone."

"Were we going to a party?"

Jake tossed him the admittance chit. "A fundraiser for the War Museum and—"

"One of my favorite causes."

"And Karla Maxfield's going to attend," continued Jake. "It's probable she knows something about what's been going on." He filled Gomez in on what he'd picked up from Sulman, adding, "I followed up on this some. Karla was indeed down there in Managua for most of the period that Maxfield, Jr. and Eve were in town."

"If she really knows anything of importance, *amigo,* she's got to be on somebody's list, too."

"Yeah, you might mention that to her. Might prompt her to confide in you."

"That coupled with the wellknown Gomez charm ought to do it."

Picking up one of the disabled listening devices, Jake tossed it in his palm a few times. "What'd you find out today?"

Gomez told him about Timecheck's report on Dr. Morgana. "Researching the lady's career on my own thereafter," added the detective, "I discovered that she's very likely been tied in with no less than five other assassinations over the past couple years."

"You come up with anything as to what Maxfield, Jr. knew? Or anything on Surrogate 13?"

"Nada, nothing at all."

"Maybe Karla Maxfield has some answers."

Leaning against the wall and folding his arms, Gomez said, "You know Alicia Bower much better than I do."

"True."

"She's really got some information to pass on—this isn't just an excuse to get you over there?"

Jake grinned. "I doubt it, Sid," he answered. "Unlike you, I don't have the sort of charm that drives women goofy."

THE SECURITY ROBOT was sitting in the hotel corridor, leaning against the wall, legs spread wide and coppery head tilted far to the right. His left eye was dangling from its socket and an acrid plume of sooty black smoke was drifting up from a large jagged rent in the top of his skull.

The door to Alicia's suite was standing nearly a foot open just beyond the slumped guard.

Drawing his stungun, Jake eased along the hallway of the Jefferson Hotel.

After listening for several seconds outside the doorway, Jake lunged and booted the door completely open.

The large living room was empty, an armchair was toppled over on its back with its legs in the air. Out the window you could see the Washington Monument glowing white in the night.

Jake stopped in the center of the big room, gun ready.

Then, slowly, he crossed to the bedroom.

No one was in there. Another chair lay upsidedown against the wall and a cosmetics case, its contents scattered, had fallen in front of it. The bedside vidphone was on the fritz, the screen glowing red and giving off harsh crackling sounds.

Beside the bed Jake noticed a fragment of paper, about two inches square. He picked it up, frowning. "Funny thing to find on her bedroom floor," he observed.

The scrap was from a very old newspaper, probably from way back in the twentieth century. His frown deepening, Jake very carefully slipped the fragment into his jacket pocket.

He went carefully through the rest of the hotel suite, but found no trace of Alicia.

15

□

THE MARTIAL MUSIC hit Gomez while he was still strolling along Independence Avenue a good block and a half from the War Museum. He was wearing the most conservative jacket he'd brought along with him from SoCal.

The five-story plastiglass, metal and neomarble building had been sprayed with red, white and blue litepaint for tonight and it glowed and flashed against the clear night. Sitting up in a huge gondola that hung suspended from a hoverliner was the Military Service Robot Band. Its brassy music, vastly amplified, flowed down across the night sky.

Several dozen people in formal attire were climbing the entrance ramp toward the high arched entryway as Gomez reached the War Museum. A pretty blonde android held up a hand in a halt gesture.

"Your ticket, please, sir."

Smiling, he handed her the plasticard Jake'd given him. "Here you are, *bonita.*"

"All in order," the android said, smiling back. "You'll be happy to know that Vice President McCracklin will be making a special holographic appearance here later tonight."

"That truly cheers me up." He continued up the ramp.

"I hope you won't think me rude," spoke a tall silvery blonde woman whom he was passing.

"I might, it's hard to say at this point."

"I wanted to ask you about your . . . um . . . coat I guess you'd call it."

"Sí?"

"What color is it?"

"Blue."

"Blue usually doesn't have flecks of . . . um . . . pink in it."

"This is," he explained patiently, "SoCal Pacific Ocean Sunset Blue, ma'am."

"Ah, yes, that explains it." Nodding, she moved away from him.

There were at least two hundred guests milling and mingling in the huge foyer. Gomez weaved his way through them, helping himself to a glass of ale from the silver tray of a passing gold-plated servobot. He moved closer to a wall and, resting one shoulder against it and sipping his ale, scanned the crowd.

This afternoon he'd phoned the Cosmos file room, read up on Karla Maxfield's background and studied several pictures of her. She was said to be a bright and feisty young woman of twenty-nine. She had dark brown hair and for the past year and a half had been working as Executive Editor for a MaxComm fax-weekly called *Gossip Digest.*

As soon as he determined Karla wasn't in the crowded foyer, he nudged his way into one of the other rooms on this level. It was the Land Tank Wing, containing sixteen tanks from previous centuries plus an animated mural of tank combat in World War II that covered one wall. The soundtrack for the mural, a combination of explosions and percussion, made this an unpopular area for conversation and there were less than fifty people here.

None of them was Karla Maxfield.

Gomez moved on. The History of Aerial Bombardment Room was even less conducive to chatting and only a dozen dedicated aviation buffs were in evidence. The Panorama of Propaganda Suite was relatively quiet and there Gomez spotted his quarry, standing with three other people in front of a display of twentieth century Uncle Sam posters.

She was wearing a full-length black gown and had a single yellow rose in her hair. There was a tall black man on her right, a thin man in his seventies on her left. The fourth member of the group was a heavyset Indian woman.

Gomez walked confidently over to them, smiling an ingratiating smile. "Good evening, Miss Maxfield," he said. "We met at—"

"You." She frowned darkly. "I know you."

"Exactly what I was saying. We met last year during a media conference in Rio," he continued. "I'm Carlos Troxa with the—"

"Bullshit," she said. "I was scanning a file on you only last month. You're Lopez . . . No, Gomez. Sidney José Gomez."

"You're confusing me, *cara,* with a notorious cousin of mine who—"

"Gomez the gumshoe," said Karla disdainfully. "Lowlife peeper, disgraced flatfoot, unscrupulous snoop who—"

"Coming from the Executive Editor of *Gossip Digest,* that remark—"

"Right, you're the doink who helped get my great friend Bennett Sands killed," she went on. "And only a few weeks ago, teaming up with that flatchested shrike, Natalie Dent, from our hated rival, Newz, you caused enormous grief for a dedicated psychiatrist named—"

"This is going to make the cordial conversation I had in mind somewhat—"

"Scram," she suggested.

The black man offered, "I can toss him out on his ear, Karla."

"No, we'll simply move elsewhere." Giving him one more glowering glance, she walked away from Gomez. "If he follows too closely on my heels, if he so much as breathes on me for the rest of the evening, then you can muss him up, Norm."

Gomez remained in place, watching the four of them depart. "I'm not," he told himself, "getting off to a very good start here."

□

TIMECHECK PUT DOWN his mug of nearcaf, rolled up his sleeve and consulted one of his bulletin watches. "Doesn't do us a heck of a lot of good, Jake, if you're two minutes fifteen seconds early and then this dwork is seven minutes forty-five seconds late," he complained.

"You sure he's the right guy for this chore?" Jake and the information dealer were sharing a booth at the back of a Snax restaurant just off Connecticut Avenue.

"Daddy, this Quatermain *lives* down under DC and he's a firstrate guide," Timecheck assured him. "His only flaw is that he's not prompt."

From up near the entrance came the sound of a robot waiter falling over. "Vagrant, am I?" growled someone.

"He's also got something of a temper." Timecheck leaned out of the booth. "Over here, Quatermain."

A large bearded man came lumbering up to them. "Told me they didn't allow beggars in here," he said, scowling darkly. He was wearing a dirt-smeared greatcoat that bore patches of several different fabrics. "Hell, a few beggars would upgrade the looks of this cesspool."

"Jake Cardigan, this is Quatermain."

The big shaggy man held out his hand. "I hope *you're* not looking for trouble, pilgrim."

Shaking hands, Jake answered, "I'm looking for somebody to guide me through the Paper Archives Catacombs under the city."

Quatermain said, "Slide over, Timecheck," and pushed onto the seat next to him. "Why—tourist?"

"Jake's a detective. I already told you about—"

"Let's hear him tell me."

Jake grinned. "Okay, I'm impressed with your toughness," he said to the big man. "You don't take any crap from anybody and you consider dirt a sign of manhood. Now, either we get down to business—because I'm in a hurry—or you can take a hike."

Quatermain sat back, studying Jake. Then he shrugged. "What are you looking for down there?" Much of the growl had left his voice.

From his pocket Jake took the scrap of newspaper he'd found in Alicia's bedroom. "This is a longshot maybe, but it seems likely this came from down there." He handed it across to the bearded man. "Someone I'm interested in was grabbed. It's possible that she was taken by somebody from the Catacombs. I want to look for her down there."

After wiping his large, flattened nose on his coat sleeve, Quatermain took the scrap between stained thumb and forefinger. "1960s, *New York Times,*" he said after a few seconds. "Likely came from the Newspaper Wing."

"I know a rich assortment of marginal citizens live down there in those tunnels and storerooms," said Jake. "Including various gangs and hoodlums for hire."

"Plus a hell of a lot of independent, creative folks," added Quatermain, scowling as he tossed the fragment in Jake's direction. "I'd hate to think you were implying that I'm a thug, pilgrim."

"You're too sweet tempered to be a thug." Putting the scrap of paper away, Jake started to slide out of the booth. "Timecheck, I'll have to find another guide. Your friend's got too many problems for—"

"I don't have problem one," Quatermain told him. "You want a guide, I'm the best there is. Just because I won't be insulted or—"

"Jake, trust me, he's just in a grouchy mood tonight," put in Timecheck. "Nobody knows the layout down there as well as Quatermain."

"Why'd they grab this ladyfriend of yours?" the shaggy man inquired.

"Not sure. Probably to keep her from talking to me."

"What motive?"

"I'm investigating a murder, one with politics and maybe Tek involved."

"There are several gangs down in the Paper Archives Catacombs who specialize in that sort of work."

"Can you get us safely there for a look around?"

"Can you pay me one thousand dollars?"

Jake said, "Okay, but only half now."

"All now," countered Quatermain. "If you get knocked off down there, I may not have time to frisk your body for the rest of my face."

16

GOMEZ WAS ON his second ale when the unexpected opportunity arose. He had, keeping a safe distance, been trailing Karla and her party through the War Museum. Norm, who Gomez concluded must be some sort of bodyguard for the communications heiress, threw him a few nasty glances but nobody had thus far tried to eject him.

It was on the second level that the incident took place. The room was devoted to robot warriors of the twenty-first and twenty-second centuries. There were fifteen formidable examples on display, each standing stiff and still atop a low pedestal.

Gomez was in conversation with a young woman who was a First Lieutenant in the Military Service. "That's an interesting point of view," he was saying to her, casually watching Karla Maxfield across the room.

"Oh, but it's absolutely true," the lieutenant told him. "Hand-to-hand combat is always much more exciting than—"

"*Chihuahua,*" exclaimed Gomez, turning away from her.

The large gunmetal robot soldier on the pedestal nearest Karla had suddenly come to life. He swung out with his heavy left arm and slapped at Norm.

The force of the blow was enough to send the black bodyguard sailing hard into the wall six feet away.

Then the robot soldier started to raise his right hand, which had a lazgun built in, and aim it at the young woman.

Gomez had yanked out his stungun. Planting his feet wide and gripping the gun in both hands, he fired at the robot.

The beam hit him in the side and the big mechanical warrior gave a spasmodic jerk.

After firing a second blast, Gomez went running toward the robot.

The robot's arms dropped to his sides. He took two wobbling steps ahead, swayed and started to topple from his pedestal.

Sprinting, Gomez grabbed Karla around the waist and dragged her out of the path of the falling mechanical soldier.

The robot smacked the floor with a resounding, rattling thump, his heavy head just missing her left foot.

Karla tried to speak to Gomez, but ended up coughing instead. Finally she was able to say, "You seem to have saved my life."

He nodded. "Apparently so." He let go of her. "Maybe now, out of gratitude, you'll do me a favor, *señorita.*"

"I owe you at least one, Gomez."

"I'd like to talk to you about your brother and Eve Bascom."

Norm was back on his feet, bracing himself against the wall. "Get the hell away from her, Gomez," he warned.

"Come by my place at eleven tonight." She leaned close, whispered her address and kissed Gomez on the cheek.

"Damn it," shouted Norm. "That's only going to encourage him."

THE PAPER ARCHIVES Catacombs had been established back early in the twenty-first century, expanding from underground space originally intended to serve as living and office space for essential government officials in the event of a nuclear attack. Gradually the underground rooms and passways had been expanded and extended, converted to store the paper ephemera of Washington. Official memos, financial records, newspapers, the spillover of the Library of Congress and tons of other paper documents all ended up beneath the city.

Sparsely patrolled by a scattering of rundown security robots

in recent decades, the Catacombs had long been used as residence and refuge space for all sorts and conditions of people—
vagrants, runaways, outlaws, artists and eccentrics.

With Quatermain guiding him, Jake began his descent by way
of an entry hole in Potomac Park.

The metal ladder rattled as they climbed down and their footfalls echoed hollowly. A chill dampness quickly closed in around
them.

"Guard on this entrance has been flooey for a year or more,"
explained the shaggy man, dropping from the last rung to the
dirty stone floor.

As Jake followed him into a long, dimlit tunnel, he noticed a
battered robot slumped against a black-stained tiled wall. One
arm was missing and a plump grey rat was perched on the guardbot's lap, dozing.

Other rats, some fat and some lean, went scurrying along the
murky tunnel ahead of them. On each side of the damp passway
rose bundles of ancient memos, boxes of faxcopies, plyosacks
stuffed with shredded documents. The rats had been at most of
the sacks and twists and tatters of long-ago secret communications lay scattered thickly underfoot.

In a niche that had been hollowed out between tottering stacks
of official records, a gaunt old woman, wrapped in what might
once have been a rug, was slumbering, hooked up to a dirty Tek
Brainbox.

"Tekheads," commented the bearded guide scornfully. "What
do they see in that crap? Reality is what you have to face in this
world."

The tunnel sloped and then forked.

Quatermain indicated the righthand branch, which was somewhat warmer and better illuminated. Man-high bundles of twentieth century newsmagazines were stacked along one side of the
downslanting tunnel.

"Wineheads coming up next," announced Jake's shaggy
guide. "Nice oldfashioned vice, this is."

Several large cluttered storerooms branched off the tunnel. In one of them, huddled around a fire made mostly of burning magazines, ten or so people in tattered clothes were passing around a plastiflask of purplish liquor.

"They like to keep together," observed Quatermain, stepping across a young woman who lay sprawled in their path, snoring vigorously. "Shared interests."

Jake paused, carefully lifted the slumbering girl and carried her over to the doorway of the storeroom. Leaving her propped at the doorway, he followed his guide deeper underground.

QUATERMAIN HELD OUT his arm to block Jake's progress. "We'll make a stop here," he said quietly.

Up on their right about a hundred feet was a large storeroom labeled BookBin 19. Bright yellowish light was spilling out of its open doorway, along with the smell of meat cooking.

"Who hangs out here?" asked Jake.

"They call themselves the Bookworms," answered the big bearded man. "Mostly in their teens—runaways and raiders. Thing is, they roam all through the Catacombs and they know just about everything that's going on."

"Then they'll know if the young woman I'm hunting for was brought down here."

Quatermain nodded his shaggy head. "And, for a fee, they'll tell us," he said. "You'll handle the fee, sport."

All at once from up ahead came a cry of pain. It sounded like a young woman.

Scowling, Quatermain pulled Jake over to a narrow tunnel that ran alongside the bookbin. "Could be something's going on wrong in there," he whispered. "We'll take us a gander before we go barging on in."

Midway along the dark passage glowed a circle of light, about the size of a plate, in the stone wall of the building.

Quatermain shuffled up to the hole, hunched and chanced a look inside. After a half a minute, he nodded and stepped back. "Take a peek."

At the center of the booklined room five young people were standing, stiffly, around a cookfire over which a small animal was roasting. A large chromeplated robot was holding a sixth youth, a thin redhaired girl of about seventeen, by the back of her jacket, dangling her about a foot above the stone floor.

A short thickset man in a dark suit was covering the rest of the youths with a lazgun.

"Nate Anger and Sunny," said Jake.

The silvery robot slapped the dangling girl across her face, which already had two red welts showing on it. She cried out again.

"One of you kids sure as hell better tell us what we want to know," suggested Anger. "Now then—where is Alicia Bower?"

17

NORM THE BODYGUARD was sitting, big arms folded across his broad chest, on a delicate silver chair in the foyer of Karla Maxfield's small waterside villa in an exclusive and highly secure section of New Baltimore. "I'm not absolutely certain," he was saying to Gomez, "that you're Gomez."

"I am," Gomez assured him, "the one and only."

Two hefty security robots, each painted an eggshell white, were holding the detective by his arms.

"I tell you," continued the large black man, "I think we better run a full check on you. I mean, for all we know, you're really an android. Possibly one of those kamikazes the Teklords are so fond of using. Stuffed full of dangerous explosives and primed to go off and destroy Miss Maxfield."

"It is possible, *pendejo,* that they really are out to do her in," said Gomez. "But hassling me is only going to—"

"A strip search, too, may be called for." Norm smiled. "We can't be too careful, considering an attempt's already been made on her life tonight."

"Too bad you weren't this clever when that bot soldier whapped you in the *cabeza,*" said the detective, trying unsuccessfully to free himself from the metallic grasp of the two guardbots.

"I feel unhappy about that, which is why I intend to be extra careful with—"

"That's about enough, Norm." Karla's angry voice came flaring out of an overhead voxbox. "Mr. Gomez is *my* guest. Send him in here at once."

"Well now, Miss Maxfield, this might not be the actual Gomez. I suggest that—"

"Send him in."

Norm sighed, shook his head, unfolded his arms, stood up, sighed again. "Okay, very well. It's on your head, dear lady." He made a dismissive gesture at the bots. "Let 'im go, guys."

Moving free, Gomez made a slight bow in the bodyguard's direction. *"Hasta luego,"* he said amiably.

He strolled up a floorlit ramp. At its end a hologram door of seeming intricately carved brass shimmered away to nothing. After Gomez crossed into a large oval living room, the door reappeared behind him.

Karla, wearing a raspberry-colored slaxsuit, was sitting in a Lucite wingchair in front of a high, narrow window that showed night and stars. "Ignore Norm," she advised. "He's something of a dwork."

"I deduced that." He settled into a plastiglass chair that was filled with pale blue water and dozens of flickering tropical fish.

"I want to thank you for what you did this evening," she told him. "And to apologize for being so rude to you earlier."

"Being rude is one of the perks of your class," he said. "Have the police or your security people determined who rigged that bot?"

"Not yet," she answered. "And really, Gomez, I'm not your ordinary rich bitch."

"Not at all ordinary, no."

"You're still ticked off at me, aren't you?"

He reflected on the question. "Maybe I am, *sí.*"

"Would you like a drink? You were drinking ale as I—"

"Gracias, but not yet, *señorita."*

"Why, by the way, do you sprinkle your conversation with— what would one call them? Mexicanisms?"

He smiled. "Growing up as a Latino in SoCal," he answered, "was not exactly endless joy. I suppose one reason is that it's a way to thumb my nose at people." His smile widened. "You're the first person to ask about it."

She smiled back. "How'd you like to come to work for Max-Comm? I think somebody like you would—"

"No, *señorita.* I'm more than content with my present station in life," he told her. "Let's get back to this attempt to do you in."

"What do you suspect?"

"That it, obviously, ties in with the death of your brother," he replied. "And the murder of Eve Bascom."

"That awful woman." She gave an angry shake of her head. "Do you think she's responsible for what happened to Arnie?"

"Other way around," he said. "Whilst he was in Managua, Nicaragua, he found out something that certain folks didn't want him to make known."

"And he tried to use that information to turn some kind of profit for himself?"

Gomez nodded. "That's a pattern of his?"

"It wasn't easy being Arnold Maxfield, Jr." His sister looked out into the night. "Arnie was never really quite up to the job. He was forever looking for ways to get ahold of big money of his own. His ambition was to start a communications network of his own—to rival my father's." She shook her head. "He never would have succeeded."

"You were down there the same time he was."

"On separate business," Karla said, "following up a report on a romance between a couple of peabrained vidwall stars for my faxweekly."

"Any idea what your brother stumbled onto?"

"Not at all. He never much confided in me."

"Somebody apparently believes he did."

"That I can't help."

Leaning forward, Gomez rested his hand on his knee. "He ever mention something called Surrogate 13 to you?"

"No—what is it?"

"*Quién sabe?* We sure don't know as yet," he said. "Who else was he especially cordial with in Managua? Somebody who could've been a source of the dangerous information he picked up?"

Karla said, "I don't know if Eve ever found out about this, but Arnie was also having an affair of sorts with a woman who teaches at the Federal Univ—"

"Ay!" He sat up. "Was it Dr. Izabel Morgana?"

"Yes, that's her." Her eyes widened. "How'd you—"

"Her name's come up before, though not in this context."

Karla told him, "Arnie always denied this, but I'm fairly certain that Izabel is tied in with the Angeles Rojos."

"The Red Angels, huh? That's the killer squad that, unofficially, takes care of enemies of the state."

"Yes, and I've been wondering if she didn't have them take care of my brother," she said. "I was sure from the beginning that his death wasn't accidental."

"We're planning to head for Nicaragua soon. Dr. Morgana is someone I'll look up."

"Approach her very carefully," she advised. "And you might find out about Dominic Hersh. He's supposedly just an Executive Diplomatic Secretary with our American Embassy. I think he's an OCC man and is pretty much running American intelligence operations in Nicaragua. Arnie had dealings with Dominic, too."

Gomez asked, "Anything else?"

"I almost wish I could head back down there with you," she said. "But I've wangled an invitation to travel for a while with President Brookmeyer's Cracker Barrel Express."

"Got a lead on some scandal?"

She smiled. "It just might be a big one."

"Details?"

"Nothing to do with your case."

"Don't let me spoil your scoop, then." He stood. "Well, *buenas noches.*"

"You're doing it again."

JAKE MOVED BACK from the spyhole, sliding out his stungun. "You carrying a weapon?" he asked Quatermain.

"I have a lazgun on me," answered the bearded guide. "But if you want any fancy shooting, that's extra money."

"Just back me up." Jake started back down the narrow alley. "I don't require anybody shot."

Inside the building the robot slapped the girl yet again.

"Somebody had better start talking," warned Anger.

Jake halted next to the doorway.

Then he leaped into the light, aimed and fired at Sunny.

The beam of the stungun shoved the robot ahead, away from the fire. He dropped the girl and she fell at his feet. As Sunny went stumbling forward, he tripped over her, went sprawling and then dropped flat out on the stone floor, disabled.

"Set down your gun, Nate," suggested Jake, stepping further into the room.

"Like hell." The OCO agent threw himself to the side. He slammed into a high bookshelf, started to swing his lazgun around to fire at Jake.

Jake dived for the floor. Before he had a chance to fire at Anger, a young man had grabbed up his own stunrifle and shot at the agent.

The beam hit him in the chest. He went bumping into the bookshelf, arms flapping. He sat abruptly, passed over into unconsciousness. A dozen or more heavy books came falling down to hit at him.

Walking over, Jake picked up the dropped lazgun. Tucking it away in a jacket pocket, he turned his attention to the fallen young woman. "How're you doing?"

"I'm okay—sort of." She accepted his hand and got, somewhat shaky still, to her feet.

The other Bookworms, gathering up their weapons, had rushed from the building and scattered.

From the doorway Quatermain inquired, "Will you be wanting any shooting now?"

"Nope." Jake turned to the young woman. She was thin, wearing a dark tunic and dark trousers tucked into black boots. "There's no reason for you to trust me, but I hope you will. I'm Jake Cardigan, with the Cosmos Detective Agency."

"My name's Janine," she said. "And, yeah, I trust you—you saved me from those two bastards."

He gestured at Sunny and Anger. "They're with the Office of Clandestine Operations," he told her. "Apparently they're hunting for the same person I am."

"Alicia Bower, would that be?"

"Is she down here somewhere?"

Janine nodded. "Yes."

"Do you know where?"

"It's not a very safe place to go, but I can take you," she offered.

"Sock him with a hefty fee," advised Quatermain.

"No charge," she said to Jake. "I owe you one."

18

QUATERMAIN MADE A grumbling sound. "This, pilgrim, is as far as I go."

They were deeper underground now, the air was mustier and the light dimmer. The rocky ground underfoot was spread with a mixture of mud and soggy shreds of paper. Lying in a puddle of stagnant water on their left was the stiff body of a long-dead cat.

"I thought this whole spread was your domain," said Jake.

"I'm not in the mood to argue," said the shaggy guide. "It's because I know these catacombs that I'm dropping off right here." He pointed ahead with a dirty hand. "Gangs, drugrunners and worse hang out down this way. I'd just as well not risk my ass any further for a lousy thousand bucks."

"Okay, we'll push on without you." Jake grinned.

Janine tapped his arm. "It's allright," she assured him. "I can get us safely to where we have to go."

The big bearded man rubbed at his bristly chin with his great-coat sleeve. "Good luck, pilgrims," he said, turning away.

GOMEZ'S SKYCAR DECIDED to land in a place he hadn't been planning to land. It went off the homeward-bound flight pattern he'd punched out about ten minutes after he'd taken off after his New Baltimore visit to Karla Maxfield.

"Hey, *loco*," he said to the controls when he realized he was being led astray. "Where we going?"

The car said nothing, simply started to drop down through the night.

Gomez tried verbal commands and button jabbing, but the vehicle had gone out of his control.

"*Mierda*," he observed as his car settle down on a nearly deserted landing lot on the outskirts of the Georgetown section of DC.

The small vidphone screen on the dash lit up. "Good evening, Mr. Gomez," said the black young woman who appeared there. "How are you?"

"Irritated, incensed, infuriated," he told her, "and generally resentful. Who the hell are you—and why'd you waylay me?"

"I'm Mr. Maxfield's swing shift executive secretary," she replied. She was seated in a grey armchair against a grey wall.

"The *late* Mr. Maxfield?"

"Oh, no. I mean Mr. Maxfield, *Senior*," the executive secretary said. "Mr. Maxfield wishes to speak to you."

"Mr. Maxfield can *vete pal carajo*," he told her. "I don't appreciate having my car plunged on into—"

"Spanish is one of the languages I speak, Gomez." A thickset blond man in his early sixties replaced the young woman on the phone screen.

"Congratulations, being multilingual is a real advantage in the modern-day world, Mr. Maxfield," he said. "Now, let me get on about my business or—"

"I wanted to have a talk with you."

"Call my executive secretary for an appoint—"

"Being surly, my boy, isn't a very smart course to take."

"So I've been told, yet—"

"Firstly, I wanted to thank you for saving my daughter's life," cut in the communications mogul. "But I wasn't especially anxious to have the world know we were talking. Hence this somewhat unorthodox arrangement."

"*Bueno*, I accept your thanks. Turn loose my car, *por favor*."

"There's one other thing."

Gomez sighed, leaning back in his seat. *"Qué?"*

"I understand that you and your partner, Jake Cardigan, are investigating the death of my son."

"No, we're looking into the death of Eve Bascom."

"They're connected, aren't they?"

"What's your opinion?"

"What I . . . How's that, Nita?" He glanced offscreen. "Excuse me, Gomez, but I've been reminded that I only have a moment or two more to talk with you right now."

"Adiós, then."

"I'd like you, without mentioning it to Walt Bascom or anyone else at Cosmos, to provide me with copies of your reports on—"

"You already have a competent detective agency working on this for you."

"I want, my boy, as much information as I can get on this matter," Maxfield said. "I'll pay you as—"

"We can't do business, *señor."*

Maxfield said, "I'll give you time to think about it," and was gone from the screen.

Unbidden, the skycar rose up and resumed its original course.

JANINE SAID, "THEY call themselves the Scavengers."

"Gang that took Alicia?" asked Jake.

"Yes, and they specialize in jobs like this," the redhaired girl continued. "They can move all over under DC. Then surface, grab someone or some piece of valuable loot and retreat down here again."

The tunnels they were traveling down through now were narrower, lower. Jake had to hunch slightly. "I don't think they kidnapped her on their own."

"No, that isn't likely." She reached out, touched his hand briefly. "Someone hired them to do it. You're going to have to keep in mind, Jake, that—well, they may've been paid to hold her down here for someone or they may just have been ordered to kill her."

"They could've done that in her hotel if this was just a murder for hire."

"Maybe not," said Janine. "They like to bring their victims down here for the slaughtering. The police rarely come this far and a body is easy to lose hereabouts."

Jake nodded, saying nothing.

The smell of mold and decay was strong.

After a few moments Janine said, "The Scavengers live in one of the newspaper storage rooms, but they usually keep their plunder and their victims in a magazine room. We'll try that first—it's about a quarter mile dead ahead."

"How many of them?"

"There's ten right now," she answered. "It varies, since they like to fight amongst themselves and that thins the ranks."

"Who runs things?"

She held up two fingers. "Rich and Nancy," she said. "A very mean couple of people, Jake."

"Can they be negotiated with?"

"You mean can you maybe buy her back from the gang?"

"Using money is sometimes the easiest way to do things."

She shook her head. "I doubt it." She slowed, sniffing at the tunnel air. "I mean, there's a slim chance, but it's likelier they'd kill you before you got to make an offer."

There was a new scent in the air. "Can we take them by surprise?"

"I know of some drainage tunnels that run under these. If we can . . ." Frowning, she stopped dead. "That's smoke, coming from up ahead."

Jake was aware of it, too. "Something's burning sure enough, and it's a lot more than a cook fire."

"No, this is bad." She took hold of his arm. "It smells like big fire—we get those down here sometimes." She shook her head. "I think it's coming from where the Scavengers are."

19

◙

THE SMOKE CAME flowing at them, white and thick. They could hear the crackling of flames, the cries of fear and panic.

Coughing, Janine took hold of his hand. "We have to go another hundred yards to hit those drainage tunnels," she said, her voice harsh.

"Can we get near where you think they're holding Alicia?"

"I'm hoping so," she answered as they started to run into the thickening swirls of smoke. "But I'm afraid it may be the magazine storeroom that's afire."

They ran, coughing, unable to see clearly.

"Here," said the girl finally. She knelt at the side of the tunnel and started to brush aside mud and tangles of paper scrap with the sides of her hands.

Jake helped her and they cleared away a square metal trapdoor set in the tunnel floor.

The smoke was rolling along the tunnel, you could feel the heat of the unseen blaze.

Jake grabbed the handle of the door and tugged.

Nothing happened.

He took hold with both hands, braced himself, pulled harder.

There was a rusty creaking and then the door popped open. Dank, damp air came rushing up and was swiftly swallowed by the swirling smoke.

"I'll go first." Janine clicked on a handlite and pointed it down into the darkness. "There's a metal ladder along the wall, see? Watch out, because it's slippery as hell."

As she started down, Jake heard rats, a large quantity of them, go skittering away below.

Jake followed her down the ladder and pulled the door down. It closed with a dull thunk.

A little of the smoke from above had made its way below, but the dominant smell was of decay.

Pointing with the thin beam of her light, Janine said, "We have to travel along that ledge there. It's pretty damned narrow, but otherwise we'd have to slosh along in the drainage channel and that's full of all sorts of muck."

Crossing to the ledge first, Jake held out his hand to her. She joined him on the ledge, which was about three feet wide.

"We're going to have to do this single file." She edged around him to take the lead.

"Is there any alarm system up there—and sprinklers in place?" he asked.

She started making her way along the narrow passage. "Some sprinklers. The alarms have been on the fritz for years," Janine answered. "Sprinklers might work, no way of telling. They do sometimes."

"What usually happens when there's a serious fire?"

"Usually we're able to get it under control ourselves. Other times, though, it just blazes away until it dies out on its own." She was walking slowly, counting off paces.

The further they went, the louder was the sound of the flames up above them. There were screams of pain, too.

Janine glanced upward. "I think the fire's in the newspaper storeroom," she told him. "Maybe it hasn't spread to the magazine space yet."

"Trouble is, we don't know which room Alicia is in."

"No, but—hold it!" She stopped still, clicked off her light.

"What?" he whispered in the new darkness.

A rattling had begun almost directly above. Creaking followed, then a metal trapdoor opened in the ceiling.

Smoke came pouring and spilling down, along with the roar of flames.

"Get your ass down there, bitch," ordered a raw male voice.

"This fire is your fricking fault. I'm going to fix you fricking good before I turn you over."

GOMEZ PACED.

The living room of the suite was wide, well suited to pacing.

"Time?" he said aloud.

"It's now seven minutes shy of one AM," replied the voxbox overhead.

Puckering his cheek, Gomez said, "I'm getting worse than Timecheck."

"Beg pardon, sir?"

"Nada." He dropped into an armchair.

A moment later the suite computer announced, "Phone call."

Gomez jumped up. "Who?"

"Walt Bascom, Greater Los Angeles."

"I'll take it," he said, moving into a chair that faced the vidwall.

"What the hell are you two dimwits up to?" began the head of the Cosmos Detective Agency.

"Can you give me a slight hint, *jefe,* as to the source of your ire?"

"You know damned well what I'm riled about, Sid," he said, angry. "I specifically told you guys not to—Where's Jake, by the way? I want him in on this."

Pointing at the floor with a thumb, Gomez said, "Under DC, far as I know. I was commencing to grow concerned just before you—"

"No matter. You can tell him what I had to say. When I sent you bumblers back there, didn't I—"

"Momentito," interupted Gomez, holding up his hand. "You just been talking to your son, am I right?"

"You're right. Richard was damned upset," said Bascom, scowling. "He told me he knew that Eve had been sleeping around and that he wasn't sure he could handle that. Why in the hell did you tell him?"

"Did Richard say we had?"

"No, but—hell, how else could he have found out?"

"Death is a great eye opener," he suggested to his boss. "He's starting to see things differently now."

"You're sure you didn't let something slip?"

"*Jefe,* you're letting personal stuff futz up your perspective," Gomez said. "You ought to know that Jake and I wouldn't doublecross you."

After a few seconds Bascom said, "Yeah, I guess that's so."

Gomez stood up, walked a few steps away from the chair. "I can," he offered, "fill you in on what we've been finding out."

"Okay, you'd better," said Bascom. "And excuse my calling you a halfwit."

"It was dimwit, but who's counting." He sat back down and started to make his report.

□

ALICIA BOWER CAME climbing down the rattling metal ladder into the drainage tunnel. Smoke and fire-tinted light came spilling down into the darkness with her. She climbed slowly, her auburn hair tangled and her face streaked with dirt and soot.

Following her down was a large, flabby man with dead-white hair. There was a lazgun tucked into his wide silvertrimmed belt.

"That's Rich," whispered Janine in Jake's ear as they stood there watching.

He had his stungun drawn and now he took the handlite from the girl.

As soon as Alicia touched the ground, Jake took two steps ahead. He clicked on the light, aiming its beam at the descending Rich. "Okay, halt right where you are," he advised. "Then, very slowly and carefully, pluck that gun out of your belt and drop it down here."

Instead Rich yelled, "Frick you!" He leaped from the metal ladder and aimed his big falling body directly at the handlite Jake was holding.

Jake started to dodge, but wasn't fast enough.

The heavy young man hit hard against him and they both went falling, off the narrow ledge and smack into the water-filled drainage channel.

The scummy water was only about two feet deep here, but Jake was shoved below the surface by the weight of the Scavenger leader.

He twisted, struggling to get out from under and up to air.

Rich stayed atop him, jabbing him in the face and chest with both big fists.

Straining, Jake brought both knees up and then kicked out.

He managed to boot Rich in the midsection and the fat man groaned and flopped back off him.

Pushing at the rocky channel floor with both palms, Jake raised himself to a standing position. He stood, swaying, gasping in air, dripping foulsmelling water.

Rich was up, too. He'd kept his lazgun in his belt and he was tugging it out.

Jake lunged, butting him hard in the stomach.

The Scavenger gave out a tremendous pained gasp and sat down in the water.

Jake moved forward and kicked.

His booted foot connected with Rich's fat chin.

The force of the kick lifted him up, made him gnash his teeth together. He fell to the left, hitting his dead-white head against the stones. Passing over into unconsciousness, Rich slowly slid down the slimy side of them and sank into the dark water.

As Jake bent to pull him out of the water, a voice from above cried, "You goddamn buttjumper! You killed him."

A lazgun crackled.

20

As JAKE TURNED to look up, he saw a thin, darkhaired young woman come falling down from the opening above.

A coppery lazgun was spinning down through the smoky air, too. It hit the ledge, bounced into the water and sank. The body of the young woman followed it an instant later, splashing up scummy water and then sinking away.

Jake started to reach for her.

"Don't bother," said Janine from the ledge. "She's dead and done for." There was a snubnosed lazgun in her left hand. "That's Nancy, his woman. She was fixing to kill you."

"Thanks." He got the unconscious Rich up out of the water and stretched him out on the ledge.

Alicia was leaning back against the wall, one hand clutching her other arm. "I was hoping you'd find me, Jake," she said quietly. "Though I didn't have much reason to believe you would."

He grinned at her, then turned to Janine. "Can we get clear of the Catacombs if we stay down here?"

"Sure, but we'll have to travel another good mile or more."

"You up to that?" he asked Alicia.

"I can do twice that to get away from this awful place," she assured him.

THEIR PROGRESS ALONG the ledge was slow. Janine, using her handlite, went first in the singlefile line. Alicia went next and finally Jake.

They'd outdistanced the smoke and the sounds of the blaze in the tunnels above.

Janine glanced back over her slim shoulder. "What'd Rich mean about you starting the fire?" she asked.

"In a way it was my fault," answered Alicia. "They took me to one of those damn newspaper storage rooms—that was after they'd broken into my hotel suite and taken me, trussed up and gagged. When they untied me, I shoved into the nearest lout and tried to run. But I was wobbly and I fell. I knocked over another of them and he fell back into their cook fire. That sent flames and grease splashing all over. Some of the dry newspapers took fire and it just turned into a blaze before they could stop it."

"Serves 'em right," observed Janine.

Something made a sudden plopping splash in the drainage channel. Janine swung the light beam over and caught a large rat in the act of swimming by.

Jake asked, "Did they say why they'd grabbed you?"

"Not exactly, but it wasn't for ransom and they weren't planning to kill me."

"What, then?"

"Rich—was that the fat one with white hair?"

"Yeah."

"Well, Rich implied they were going to hold me there until someone else came to collect me."

"Any idea who the someone else was?"

"No, and I tried to wheedle that out of him," she said. "He was exactly, though, the sort you can cajole."

"Where was he planning to take you when he forced you down here?"

"I'm not sure, Jake. After the fire got out of hand, he dragged me along with him," said Alicia. "I imagine he was going to try to get me to a safe place, then contact whoever it was that hired him."

After a moment Jake asked her, "Who knew you were going to be meeting with me?"

"Nobody."

"That vidphone you called me from wasn't tapproof, was it?"

She said, "No, I guess not. But why—"

"Not sure. You didn't confide in anyone else?"

"I mentioned to my attorney, Kay Norwood, that I'd be contacting you when I got to DC. But she's a longtime friend."

"What I'm trying to figure out is whether this has anything to do with the case we're working on," he told her. "Or if it's just a coincidence that you were abducted right before I was due to drop in on you."

"It might tie in with what you're investigating," Alicia said. "That's why I wanted to see you. Does Surrogate 13 mean anything to you?"

He stopped. "It does, yeah," he said.

THE SAFE HOUSE was in Arlington, Virginia. Jake got Alicia there at a few minutes after three AM. As soon as they entered the small black-and-white living room, the auburnhaired young woman put her arms around Jake and kissed him.

Stepping back, she said, "Thanks."

"You're welcome," he said. "Cosmos will have operatives watching you while you're here and escorting you around DC on your Mechanix business. It's possible, though, if this does tie in with our case, that you'll be safe soon as they comprehend that you've told me what you know."

"Or they might decide to kill us both."

"That," he conceded, "is another possibility, yeah."

"Snug," she remarked, glancing around the room. "Do you think there'd be any clothes here that'll fit me?"

"There are wellstocked wardrobe closets in both bedrooms," he answered. "Take your pick. All part of the Cosmos service."

"Then I'll go clean up and change," she said, nodding at him. "And maybe you ought to as well, you think?"

Jake looked down at his soggy clothes and at the muddy footprints his waterlogged boots had made on the grey thermocarpet. "That's a terrific suggestion," he said, grinning.

"Thanks for everything, Jake." She moved close to him, kissed him again and then turned away. "Saving my miserable life is getting to be a habit with you."

21

THE BEDSIDE VIDPHONE buzzed.

Gomez, who'd been lightly dozing, sat up in bed. "Lights," he requested.

The room obliged, soft light blossomed overhead.

"Time?"

"5:49."

"Gracias," said the tousled detective. "I'll take the call now."

It wasn't Jake who appeared on the small phonescreen. "You look groggy," observed the heavyset Sergeant Ramirez. "And you seem to be sleeping alone. *Por qué?"*

"You forget I'm a loyal husband," said Gomez, smoothing down his tangled hair. "Is this call just a moral bedcheck or do you have some other reason for this unseemly invasion of my privacy?"

"I'm calling you on a tapfree phone," said the Manhattan policeman. "Are things secure at your end?"

"Sí, I swept the whole suite before toddling off to bed."

Nodding, Ramirez continued. "Couple hours ago I heard from Charley Charla, the famous informant. He claimed he had about five hundred bucks' worth of important information for you. Charley'd been trying to contact you, wasn't having any luck."

"Ay, I forgot to put his name on the Cosmos call forwarding list. Any idea what Charley has for me?"

"Yeah, he passed it on to me, since he was planning to go on an immediate sabbatical."

"He's in trouble, is he?"

"We'll come to that, Sid," said the cop. "Charley suggested you contact an *hombre* named Dreamer Garcia, who's to be found in Managua, Nicaragua. Seems this Dreamer has some vital stuff about certain activities of the Joaquim Tek Cartel to pass along. The five hundred dollars was for Charley's tip—Dreamer Garcia wants an additional one thousand."

"I notice you're using the past tense in alluding to my informant."

"Exactly, *amigo*. Poor Charley was found—most of him anyway—up in Spanish Harlem a half hour ago. A couple of lazrifles turned him into a pretty messy jigsaw puzzle."

"*Dios.*"

"I'd attempt to tread very lightly from this point," advised his police friend. "In fact, you'd be smart to stay the hell away from Central America altogether."

"Nope, Roberto, I can't let a little thing like a brutal assassination scare me off," Gomez told him. "My reputation as a fearless op would suffer, not to . . . Oops! I have to sign off now. *Adiós.*"

Gomez had become aware of footfalls out in the living room of their suite.

He swung off the bed, grabbed up his trousers from where he'd tossed them and hopped into them.

Picking up his stungun, he opened the bedroom door and peered out.

Jake was standing by one of the windows, watching the night fading away toward dawn.

"Is all well, *amigo?*" He set his gun on the coffee table.

"Sure, yeah."

"You sound glum."

Jake turned away from the window. "You got the message I asked the agency to send along?"

"That you'd rescued Alicia Bower from some goons and were escorting her to a place of refuge, *si.*" He settled into an armchair. "I assumed you'd be spending the rest of the night with her."

"So did Alicia."

"How come you didn't?"

Jake shrugged. "I must still be in mourning."

"Ah, would that I had the opportunity to turn down romantic propositions from heiresses." Gomez sighed. "Best offer I got from *my* heiress, the glamorous Karla Maxfield, was for gainful employment."

"Doing what?"

"Come to think of it, *amigo,* I'm not sure if she wants me to be a crackerjack newshound or a stalwart bodyguard. I, in my usual charming manner, rejected the offer."

Turning his back to the window, Jake asked, "Find out anything from her?"

"Well, you can add Karla to the list of folks who didn't especially care for Eve Bascom," answered his partner. "Of more interest is the fact that her late *hermano* was keeping company with none other than Dr. Izabel Morgana."

"You mean now—at the same time he was fooling around with Eve?"

"*Sí,* apparently whilst Eve was cheating on her hubby, Junior was cheating on her with a formidable lady who's chummy with the Red Angels death squads."

"That makes for an interesting triangle."

Gomez nodded in agreement. "Karla is of the opinion that a gent named Dominic Hersh, who seemingly holds a mid-level position with our esteemed embassy in Managua, is more than likely an OCO agent."

"How's he tie in with her brother?"

"Arnie and Hersh did some socializing during his sojourn down there."

"We'll look into the guy. Anything else?"

"Karla seems to have no notion as to who knocked off her brother, but she's certain his death was not an accidental one."

"Any reason for her believing that?"

"None that she's confiding. My impression is that it's a gut feeling sort of thing," said Gomez with a shrug. "Finally, alas, she knows absolutely *nada* about Surrogate 13."

"That's okay, I found out what Surrogate 13 is."

Gomez sat up. "Alicia told you?"

"That's what she wanted to talk to me about, yeah."

"Did she journey here from the West just to rendezvous with you?"

"No, she's in DC on Mechanix International business. But when she found out I was here, she called."

"So Surrogate 13 must be something they made on the sly at her late *padre's* robot and android works. *Verdad?"*

Jake moved to the sofa and sat down. "It was, yeah, a secret project that her father and some of his OCO friends initiated," he said, leaning back. He looked weary, there were faint shadows beneath his eyes. "That was a few months before Owen Bower died. Alicia, with the help of her attorney, found information about Surrogate 13 in the Mechanix archives. That was a couple days ago, stuff the crooks at the top hadn't had a chance to erase before the roof fell in on them."

"So what the blazes is Surrogate 13?"

"An android simulacrum, a much more sophisticated one than anything they've turned out to date."

"Sim of what?"

"The President of the United States—Warren Brookmeyer."

"Ah, that president." Gomez scratched at his moustache. "And who ordered this dupe of the prez?"

"Nothing about that was left in the records," answered Jake. "Alicia knows it was completed and shipped somewhere about a week before her father died. But not where."

"Those *cabróns* at Mechanix, the bunch we tangled with during our other case—they were in cahoots with all sorts of shabby folks in and out of the government."

"Which is why we don't know as yet if this android dupe of Brookmeyer went into the White House or somewhere else altogether," said Jake. "Nor do we have any idea who got the project rolling in the first place."

"Why'd Alicia think you'd be interested in what she'd unearthed about Surrogate 13?"

Jake said, "That's an interesting question."

"And does it, *amigo,* have an interesting answer?"

"Her attorney, Kay Norwood, suggested to her that I ought to be filled in on the Surrogate 13 business. Norwood told her it might tie in with the case you and I are working on."

"How'd the lawyer know that?"

"She didn't pass along any details to Alicia, so I was eager to ask her directly, Sid," replied Jake. "She's not, however, at her home or office out in the Topanga Sector and nobody seems to have any idea of what's become of her."

Gomez narrowed his left eye. "Could the fair Alicia be holding anything back?"

"Nope, she's not," Jake assured him. "She's about the only person involved in this mess that I think I can trust."

"Speaking of the prexy of this great land of ours," said Gomez, swallowing a yawn, "here's another small coincidence. Karla Maxfield is going to be covering Brookmeyer's Cracker Barrel extravaganza for her gossip rag."

"So is a multitude of media types."

"The lass implied that she was onto some scandal involving the president, though, Jake," said his partner. "Maybe Brook-meyer had an andy replica of himself made up for some scandalous reason."

"And maybe all she's interested in is some shady spacetech deal his brother pulled off ten years ago," Jake said. "Right now, though, the place to look for answers is down in Nicaragua."

"I was about to suggest that very course of action," said Gomez and told Jake what Sergeant Ramirez had passed along to him.

"We'll head down there tomorrow."

"*Mañana* it is." Gomez stretched up out of his chair. "But let's make every effort not to have an accident."

DOMINIC HERSH WAS small for his age. Barely, if he really stretched and stood tall, four foot eleven. His mother assured him he needn't worry. He'd shoot up, probably long before his fourteenth birthday next year, and be as tall as his brothers. They were both over six feet.

That didn't help any now, though.

He shivered, though he struggled not to, as he walked along the high grey main corridor of the Administration Building of the Willingham Military Academy. His uniform itched and it was too big by at least a full size. When he complained about it, they told him he'd grow into it.

The afternoon outside was bleak, with snow falling steadily and a strong bitter wind blowing down across the sloping fields that surrounded the isolated academy buildings.

"Double-time it, mister," ordered the huge uniformed robot who popped now out of the doorway of the Detention Centre to glower at him with his plastiglass eyes. "You were due here at 16:00 hours on the dot. What time is it, mister?"

Swallowing, Hersh halted and, as smartly as he could, saluted. "I don't know, sir."

"You don't know, Cadet Hersh? Why don't you know?"

"Somebody swiped my watch, sir."

"What's that? Speak up, mister, I can't hear you when you whisper like a baby."

"Oh, screw you, you son of a bitch!" shouted the boy.

"What's that?" The stunned military robot took a shocked step backward. "Do you know whom you're . . . awk!"

Hersh, his small hand shaking, had whipped out the lazgun he'd been carrying concealed under his tunic. He fired it, sending a crackling beam of intense light right into the big robot's broad chest.

The spear of light slashed the torso nearly in half, from left to right.

Gears and wires, bulbs, circuit boards—all came erupting out of the smoking gap in the chest.

"How do you like *that,* mister?" Hersh laughed, dodging out of the way as the uniformed robot toppled to the floor.

Before the fallen robot had ceased rattling, the boy knelt beside him. He put the lazgun close to the mechanism's left eye and fired again.

The entire metal head exploded, vomiting shards of glittering metal and a multitude of gears and gadgets, sending all that technical crap sliding and skidding across the highly polished floor of the Detention Centre office.

"You rotten little bastard! What have you done now?"

Colonel Gaines, the head of the whole damned academy, was standing there. A large black man, whose uniform fit him perfectly.

Smiling, Hersh held up the lazgun he was clutching. "You know, I never liked the idea of one of you people running this place, sir," he told him. "What say we fix that, okay?"

He fired into the colonel's face.

The head vanished and bright morning sunlight filled the halls of the Ad Building.

Hersh gave a contented sigh.

He opened his eyes and was puzzled. He couldn't quite remember where he was supposed to be.

Jesus, that was happening too often lately. But wait a minute. It wasn't all that serious. Who'd told him that?

Dr. Hedley. That's right, Dr. Hedley had assured him that his degree of habituation wasn't especially dangerous. And reliving, but revising, the bad times in his youth actually had a therapeutic value.

"Not dangerous at all." Hersh sat up in the big comfortable chair at the center of his large den. Very carefully he removed the Tek headset, placing it and the Brainbox on the realwood table beside him.

"Nicaragua," he said aloud. "Yes, I'm in Managua, Nicaragua." He frowned, concentrating harder. "I'm sitting in my den. This is my house and I live on . . . What's the street? I'll get it." The frown deepened, lines formed around his mouth. "Of course, on the Avenida La Emboscada."

Hersh laughed, pleased with himself. The Tek sessions weren't going to do him any permanent harm. No matter what they said, you could use Tek safely if you were careful and disciplined about it.

Rising, he gently gathered up the Tek gear and the small opaque box of Tek chips. He hid that all away in the usual hiding place. He smoothed his thinning hair and glanced at the gilt-framed mirror behind his desk. He was five foot eight. Certainly not tall, but not short either.

The vidphone sounded.

"Who is it?" he asked, moving around behind his wide metal desk and sitting in the comfortable chair.

"Frank Dockert," the phone told him.

"That asshole," Hersh muttered. "Okay, connect him."

The heavyset black man appeared on the screen. "Are you ill, Dominic?"

"Not in the least, but it's very thoughtful of you to call all the way from DC to find out, Frank."

Dockert said, "It's possible that you've fried your brains beyond repair with all that Tek you do. I have to tell you that I'm getting damned tired of the snotty way you—"

"Do you have anything else to tell me?"

"Jake Cardigan and Sid Gomez are enroute to Managua. They left the Manhattan Skyport roughly an hour ago."

"Persistent bastards, aren't they?"

"I don't consider these two very serious threats to anything," said Dockert. "But others do, so I'm alerting you."

"I'll take care of them, Frank."

"Try to do it a little more subtly than your usual job."

"Goodbye, Frank." He ended the call and stood up. "Seems like they're everywhere these days." His right hand tightened around the trigger of an imaginary lazgun.

22

THE SOFTLIT GREY corridor was full of loud mournful organ music and it reeked of flowers. Taking two careful steps forward the chromeplated robot in the black suit and grey gloves held out his hand. "Allow me to express our sympathy at your loss, Mr. Bascom," he said in a polite whisper.

"What?" Richard frowned at the mechanical man. "I can't hear you with that damned music booming."

"Oh, I'm terribly sorry." He slid his lefthand glove partially off his sparkling metal wrist, pressed at the small control panel embedded there. "Perhaps the hymns are a bit loud."

The music diminished in intensity.

"Which room is the funeral service in?" asked Richard, taking out a plyochief and rubbing at his nose.

"Go ahead and sob freely, sir. We find it—"

"I'm not sobbing. The smell of flowers makes me—"

"I'm terribly sorry, sir." He tapped his wrist again and fresh air replaced the thick flowery scent. "Allow me, as I was saying, to welcome you to the Riverside Crematorium & Columbarium. In your hour of need, we feel we can serve you in—"

"Which room is my wife in?"

The darksuited robot touched gloved fingers briefly to his lips. "Allow me, if I may, to correct a possible misunderstanding, sir," he said. "Your wife, the late Eve Scanlon Bascom—a lovely name, I might mention—your wife, sir, is not actually in Mourning Room 3."

"Where the hell is she, then?"

Bowing his silvery head, the mechanism replied, "We've found, during years of faithful service, that it's much better to do the actual cremating *before* any of the mourners arrive for the service. Some people react very—"

"What are you talking about? You mean her body has already been—"

"At seven-thirty AM this morning, sir."

Richard grabbed hold of the robot's arm. "Damn it, nobody told me about that."

"Allow me to point out that you're not actually paying for this service." He pulled free. "Mrs. Bascom's last rites are covered by the Larson-Dunn Employees Insurance & Burial Plan."

"I still should've been told. Now I'll never see her again or—"

"Not in this world, no. Yet many believe that—"

"Never mind. What room did you say?"

"Mourning Room 3," answered the robot. "At the end of the corridor on your left, sir. You'll find quite a crowd has already gathered."

"A crowd?"

"At least a half dozen of your wife's friends and colleagues, plus the standard fifteen android mourners, provided at no extra cost, by us."

"When does the service start?"

"In exactly seven minutes, sir."

Nodding, Richard walked stiffly along the hall and into the indicated room.

There was a small dais at the front of the small dim room. Resting on a low pedestal was a pewter urn, illuminated by a small overhead spot.

Sitting up in the front row were Andre Larson and a plump blonde woman Richard thought might be one of Rosco Dunn's private secretaries.

"Good morning, Mr. Bascom." Detective Busino, wearing a dark suit, was standing just inside the door.

"Why are you here?"

"Nothing official. I just like to attend the funerals of victims in my cases."

"Are the police still investigating my wife's death?"

"No, we've written the whole thing off as an accident, sir, and shut the file up tight," answered the detective. "It would be a good idea if you do the same, if you ask me."

"Is that a warning?"

Shaking his head, Busino said, "Only a friendly suggestion."

"We aren't *friends,* so keep your—"

"Don't get upset, Mr. Bascom. At a time like this, when things look at their worst, you don't want to add to your anxiety," the detective advised. "It takes time for a wound like this to heal, but—"

"Sure, yeah. Thanks." He went over and sat in a rear seat.

"Richard, may I have a word?" Harold Allen, dean of the Lit Department, was standing in the aisle, leaning sympathetically in his direction.

"I didn't notice you were here."

Dean Allen was a tall, thin man. He settled into the seat next to him and put a hand on Richard's shoulder. "All of us in the Lit Department and most everyone at Campus Twenty of the Tri-State EdSystem want you to know how deeply saddened we are by this."

"I appreciate that."

The dean lowered his voice. "There is, however, something I must convey to you, Dick," he said. "The feeling is that the notoriety of a full-scale investigation into Eve's unfortunate accident would cause a great deal of problems."

"For whom?"

"Well, for the college in general *and* for certain important people who have an interest in our financial situation."

"Is somebody putting pressure on you, Harold?"

"Not at all," the dean told him. "But I want you to understand that if you keep this up, using a detective agency and all that, you'll be annoying factions that shouldn't be annoyed."

"So you want me to call the investigation off?"

"I don't personally, yet I want you to understand how important it is that you go no further with it."

"I don't see what business—"

"There's one other thing, Richard. Unless you comply, I may not be able to guarantee you a job at Campus 20."

"Drop it or I'm fired?"

The dean nodded slowly. "I'm afraid that's the situation."

"Well, you *and* all my friends and colleagues can go screw yourselves." Standing, he grabbed up Dean Allen by the front of his coat and shoved.

Making a surprised sputtering sound, Allen went stumbling across the aisle.

"That goes for you, too," Richard told Detective Busino as he went striding out of the room.

In the hallway the music was loud again, the smell of dead flowers strong.

THIS WAS DR. Marchitelli's day off from the Bergstrom Clinic. He was flying his skycar through the hazy sky above Miami Slum. As usual, there were several buildings afire down in the ramshackle sprawl of abandoned condos and minimalls.

His dashboard voxbox suddenly spoke. "This is a Restricted Zone."

The short, slim psychiatrist looked out to his left to see a Miami Air Police skyvan flying parallel to him. "I do volunteer work in the Miami Slum Hospice once a week," he said into his dashmike. "My special permit number is encoded on my tail tags."

"Oh, yeah, we see it now. Sorry, doctor." The police van banked and dropped away.

After landing in the small rutted lot behind the shabby two-level hospice, Marchitelli didn't go immediately inside. Instead, he stood beside his crimson car and glanced around.

Over near the lopsided security shack he spotted the bright silver skycar he'd been told to look for. Nodding, the doctor went walking over to it.

The passenger side door opened with a crisp snap. "Dr. Marchitelli, how are you?"

He bent, narrowing his eyes to look into the shadowy interior. "You're Agent Ferman from the Federal Internal Security Office?"

"Yep, that's me," answered Frank Dockert. "Get in, if you would."

Dr. Marchitelli eased into the seat and the door flipped shut on him. "I'm extremely upset about what I suspect is going on," he told the heavyset black man. "That's the reason I, very carefully, contacted you and not the Office of Clandestine Operations."

"We understand that, doctor. You only hinted at certain irregularities over the vidphone; can you give us some specifics now?" Dockert activated the engine and the car began to rise up into the hot, blurred day. "We'll fly around while we talk. Makes our little conversation more private."

"You know about the president, about what's really going on?"

"We're aware that he's a secret patient at the Bergstrom Clinic, being treated for his Tek addiction," answered Dockert. "This is a very serious matter and our agency may well have to issue a report—even though it may shake the confidence of the nation."

"The problem is, Agent Ferman, I'm convinced something else is going on."

"What do you mean?"

"It has to do with the way President Brookmeyer is being handled during his stay." He paused to run his tongue over his upper lip. "I've been involved in this very delicate situation for quite some time. You may not know this, but I was the one who explained to the president how things would go once he was brought into the clinic. Dr. Bergstrom and I worked out all the details. I don't completely approve of keeping his addiction a secret, yet I can understand—"

"Can you be more specific about what you think is wrong, doctor?"

"In the first place, Agent Ferman, I'm nearly certain they're not actually treating Brookmeyer for his addiction," he said. "I was taken off the case almost as soon as the president arrived. Then, when I complained to Dr. Bergstrom about what I'd been hearing was going on—he issued orders that I was not to go near the area of the clinic where the president is being held. And he is being held—in a ward usually reserved only for violent patients."

Dockert nodded slowly. "This is very serious indeed, doctor. Do you have any idea why our president is being kept a prisoner?"

"Not yet, but I intend to find out."

"Yes, I was afraid of that," said Dockert. "And I suppose if you don't get any satisfaction from our agency, you'll go to another. You may even alert the media."

"I'd have to, yes."

"No, actually, doctor, you won't do anything like that," said Dockert, smiling thinly. "No, unfortunately, you're going to be done in by a crazed Tek addict out for money."

"What in the hell are you—"

"But, as most people will say, that's what you get for doing charity work in a shithole like this." He kept smiling as he drew a small lazgun out of his coat.

Marchitelli twisted in his seat, trying to get free of the safety straps. "You can't—"

"Oh, sure, I can." He fired the gun.

A few moments later Dockert put in a call to Vice President McCracklin. "Everything is just fine again," he said and hung up.

23

□

THERE WAS A high, hot wind blowing across the Malibu Sector of
Greater Los Angeles. Walt Bascom was leaning back in a wingchair, his saxophone resting across his lap, watching the skycars
outside dip and sway as they fought against the heavy wind. The
people on the pedramps were walking at odd, slanted angles and
some sort of sparkling grit was drifting and swirling through the
midmorning sky.

"Informant on Holostage 2," announced the voxbox over on
his desk.

"Pertaining to what?" asked Bascom.

"The death of Eve Bascom."

Standing, the chief of the Cosmos agency set his sax across the
chair. "Who is it?"

"Harry the Tipster."

Bascom frowned and rubbed at his close-cropped hair. "Allright, connect him."

Harry, smiling broadly with his goldplated teeth, materialized
on the hologram platform across the big office. He was short,
thin and dapper. His suit was made of a plastifabric that glowed
an electric blue, the carnation in his lapel was made of polished
chrome. "How they hanging, Wally?"

" 'How they hanging, Mr. Bascom, sir,' if you please, Harry.
What sort of shabby con are you attempting on me this time?"

Holding up his small left hand, on which glittered four large
neon rings, Harry the Tipster made a be-patient gesture. "Easy

now, Mr. B, easy. In this instance I'm merely the bearer of an important message," he explained. "I have no info for sale whatsoever. If, however, you'd like to telefax a small honorarium in my direction, I wouldn't—"

"What's the message, Harry?"

"Your presence is requested at seven this very evening," said the dapper informant, "at Shinzoo's Lighthouse. That's an intimate bistro specializing in antique jazz and located in—"

"It's a pesthole in the Venice Sector of GLA," cut in Bascom. "Who's trying to lure me there?"

"Nix, nix," said Harry, looking offended. "You know I'd never be a party to your being led up the garden path, Walter. I'm passing along word from someone who's most anxious and eager to get together with you."

Bascom asked, "Who is it and why can't they come here to the Cosmos building?"

"Too risky," answered Harry. "This particular frill is lying low, as it were, in fear of her life."

"The Lighthouse is a lousy place to look for security and safety."

"Shinzoo happens to be a client of hers," the informant explained. "He has excellent facilities for hiding folks out until they can arrange to relocate elsewhere in gentler climes and—"

"Is this particular lady an attorney?"

"That's correct, you got it, Wally."

"We're talking about Kay Norwood, then, Alicia Bower's friend?"

"I'm not at liberty to divulge her identity," said the Tipster. "If I were, though, I'd be nodding my noggin in the affirmative about now."

"What does she know about the death of my son's wife?"

"Enough apparently to make certain parties eager to snip her lifeline."

"What exactly?"

"Alls I know, Mr. B, is that the quiff's got important info she thinks you ought to pass on to Jake Cardigan," answered Harry the Tipster. "Oh, and if you happen to be chinning with Jake, give him a friendly howdy from me and mention that he still owes me two hundred clams for some confidential news I passed along to him way last—"

"Okay, I'll keep the appointment, Harry." Bascom scowled at the projection of the dapper little man. "Keep in mind that if anything gets futzed up, Harry, I'll know how to find you."

"I surely hope you know where I am. Otherwise you wouldn't be able to send me a little bonus." Chuckling, Harry faded away.

THE ASSASSINATION ATTEMPT took place in the huge domed lobby of the Managua Plaza Hotel. Jake and Gomez had just stepped in out of the rainy twilight, following the turquoise-enameled bellbot who was carrying their suitcases.

There were nearly a hundred people in the wide oval lobby, sitting, wandering, coming and going. Real potted palms, an even two dozen of them, ringed the area and at its center was a broad and impressive holographic pond with glittering goldfish flashing in it. Out beyond the rainsplashed plastiglass windows you could see Lake Managua spreading out a quarter of a mile downhill.

"Very ritzy," observed Gomez, glancing around as they followed in the wake of their decorative robot. "And note the very interesting local *señorita* reclining on yonder sofa."

"You haven't got time for fraternizing," Jake reminded him.

"I've always got time for ogling," said Gomez. "Besides, she's obviously—*Ay!*" Halting suddenly, he held out a restraining arm to halt his partner.

Over near the registration desk a short, greying man had just placed his right hand on the palmprint recogpad. From a side entrance to the big lobby five men had come running. They wore black clothes, crimson berets and darktinted plastiglass face masks.

Two of the masked men aimed stunguns at the greyhaired

man. Both of the sizzling beams hit him, one in the spine, the other in the ribs. He straightened up jerkily, like a jumping jack, arms flapping high. Tottering two steps back, he toppled over, landing hard on his right side.

Another masked man, heaviest of the group, ran over to the fallen man. He had a lazgun in his fist and he started to bend over the unconscious figure.

"Nope, you don't." Jake had yanked out his stungun and he fired it now as the assassin was about to shoot the man in the head.

Jake's shot snapped him up stiff, seeming, for a few seconds, to crucify him in the air. Two of the other masked men caught him before he fell and the whole group went running out into the rainswept dusk.

Jake slipped his stungun away. "What exactly was that?"

"Probably not a smart move on your part, *amigo*," answered his partner. "Although I was about to try the same thing."

"That was a bunch of Red Angels, huh?"

"Members in good standing of the local death squads, *sí*." Gomez nodded. "I'm pretty certain their target is a gent named Ignacio Mentosa. He used to write for *La Prensa* and lecture at one of the universities hereabouts."

Two bellbots and an android desk clerk had gathered around Mentosa's unconscious body. *"Medico!"* shouted the immaculate android. *"Pronto!"*

Gomez mentioned, "If we weren't on the *Angeles Rojos* shitlist prior to this, we sure are now."

"Could this Mentosa be tied in with anything we're working on?"

"Doubt it, Jake. I heard he was coming back to Nicaragua for a few lectures. The government allows a little polite dissent now and then." He shrugged. "Obviously, however, they'd just as well Professor Mentosa didn't speak out—ever."

"On the contrary, *señores*." A slim man in his early forties had risen from a nearby real-leather armchair and was approaching them. A jagged red scar snaked down across his left cheek.

Gomez muttered, "This *hombre* smells like the law."

The man bowed slightly. "I am Captain Carlos Dacobra of the National Security Police." He smiled at them in turn. "You, of course, are Jake Cardigan and Sid Gomez of the respected Cosmos organization. I won't bother to request your ID packets or gun permits, gentlemen, since I'm more than certain everything is in order."

"Are you here to welcome us," inquired Jake, "or just to get a ringside seat for the murder of Professor Mentosa?"

Laughing, Captain Dacobra reached into his jacket. He drew out a pearlhandled lazgun. "We don't tolerate public killings, Señor Cardigan," he assured him. "Had you not acted so swiftly to avert the tragedy, I would have dealt with those Red Angels much more harshly."

"Couldn't you get in a shot while they were hightailing it out of here?"

The lawman gestured at the crowded lobby with his free hand. "Most difficult to bring down fleeing assassins without risking injuring innocent bystanders," he explained. "A great many innocent bystanders come to grief in our city as it is, gentlemen. I'm certainly not eager to add to their number."

"We're not bystanders," said Jake.

"Nor especially innocent," added Gomez.

Smiling, Dacobra said, "I did indeed come by, Señor Cardigan, to welcome you to our beautiful capital city. You may have heard that Nicaragua is a violent, lawless land and that our government is little more than a bloody dictatorship. Such, however, is not the case."

"I doubt Professor Mentosa would agree with you." Gomez nodded over at the white-enameled medibots who were, gently, loading the stunned man onto a wheeled stretcher.

"Possibly, but that is his privilege, Señor Gomez," said the captain. "If I may be of any help during your stay, contact me at once. Oh, and let me add that the Red Angels can be an extremely vengeful group. You'd best be on your guard while in Managua, *señores.*"

Jake told him, "We're always on our guard, Captain. Thanks for your interest in our welfare, though."

"De nada." He bowed again, smiled again and, turning crisply on his heel, went walking away from them.

"Chihuahua," remarked Gomez. "This has been quite a reception."

"Yeah," agreed Jake, "with fireworks and everything."

24

WALT BASCOM, WEARING one of his less rumpled suits, approached the neontrimmed doorway of Shinzoo's Lighthouse in the Venice Sector. It was a ramshackle place, sprawled just above a narrow stretch of darkening beach. Down on the sand a gaggle of scruffy youths was gathered around a crackling cookfire, barbecuing what appeared to be a small dog. Up on the slanting roof of the nightclub an ailing seagull was staggering around and producing mournful awking sounds.

A husky cyborg doorman moved out of the shadows of the recessed entryway to bar Bascom's progress. "Help you, pal?"

"I'm expected."

The large man rubbed at his stubbled chin with his coppery left hand as he scanned the detective chief. "By whom, pal?"

"A lady."

The doorman's shaggy eyebrows rose. "What's your tag?"

"Bascom."

"Hold on a sec." He activated the phone built into his metal hand. "Anybody expecting a sartorial mess called Bascom?"

The speaker in the center of his palm instructed, "Send him down to Level X, Rollo."

"Right you are." The doorman gave Bascom a curt nod. "What you want to do, pal, is go inside the club, use the door marked Private, wait until the floor opens. Follow the arrow. You got that?"

"That I do, Rollo."

As he moved aside, the big man asked, "Was the inflection you gave my name meant in derision, pal?"

Bascom paused, gave a thoughtful look up overhead. "Now that you mention it, Rollo, it just could've been," he admitted. "The thing is, trust me, you don't want to pursue the matter."

After studying him for a few silent seconds, Rollo said, "Probably not. Allright, go on inside. I was, if it's any of your goddamn business, named after my grandfather."

There were forty some patrons in the dimlit club, scattered at the small square tables, drinking, talking, some watching the rickety bandstand. Up on that, four android musicians, built to simulate jazz performers of the twentieth century, were playing "My Funny Valentine."

"A grand old tune," observed Bascom, and, warily, opened the Private door. He entered a short, deadend corridor and the door shut at his back.

"Who?" asked a thin, tinny voice from the speaker in the buff-colored ceiling.

"Bascom—same as I was out front."

"Take a couple of steps back so you'll clear the trap door," advised the voice. "And don't be such a smartass."

Bascom complied with the first part of the request.

Whirring, a little over half of the floor slid away.

A downslanting ramp was visible now, an arrow of red light throbbing at his feet.

When Bascom stepped on the ramp, the glowing arrow began moving slowly downward.

It led him some five hundred paces underground before clicking off and leaving him in complete darkness.

An image began glowing a few feet ahead of him. It coalesced into a very large Japanese man dressed in a handsome scarlet suit embroidered with golden cherry blossoms. "Just popped by to say hello, Walt," said the holographic figure, smiling and waving his right hand.

"Evening, Ray. You're looking well—for you."

Ray Shinzoo said, "I always looked great. And, listen, I weigh exactly what I did back when I was the Zero-G Wrestling champ of the world."

"So did you ask me here to admire what terrific shape you're in? Or is Kay Norwood actually down here somewhere?"

"She's here right enough," the former wrestler informed him. "First, since you're a known jazz buff, tell me what you think of the group upstairs. That Chet Baker andy cost me plenty. And that's Hampton Hawes on piano. Did you ever—"

"I prefer twentieth-century East Coast Jazz to West Coast stuff, Ray. Where's the lady?"

"C'mon, Chet Baker transcends coasts," insisted the proprietor. "Anyway, I got to go. See that you do right by my mouthpiece."

"That I shall."

Shinzoo blurred, faded and was gone.

Pale yellow light filled the hallway and a door materialized in the wall. It clicked twice before sliding open.

Bascom hesitated for a few seconds, shoulders slightly hunched, eyes narrowed, before stepping into the next corridor.

KAY NORWOOD WAS tall, less than an inch shy of six feet, and blonde. In her middle thirties somewhere, wearing a plain grey slaxsuit. She sat in one of the small blank room's two metal chairs, hands folded in her lap, knees pressed tight together. "You have an ambiguous reputation, Bascom," she told him.

He was sitting facing her, with about five feet of chill, artificial air separating them. "Just about everything you hear about me is true," he said. "You, on the other hand, have either an excellent public relations outfit working in your behalf or you actually are shrewd, brilliant and stainless."

"Both." Kay unfolded her hands, refolded them again. "Now here's the situation—I'm certain that my death has been ordered."

"And you know who?"

She nodded. "It's a team effort actually. A couple of Central American Tek cartels and certain people in one of our government intelligence agencies. I realize, yes, that this sounds sort of paranoid. The person who warned me, though, is someone I trust."

"Does this person know that you're holed up down here?"

"No, because I guess I don't trust him *that* much."

Leaning forward, Bascom rested his palm on the wrinkled right knee of his rumpled suit. "I can put you up someplace that's a hell of a lot safer than Ray Shinzoo's basement," he promised. "Is that what you need?"

"Yes, I'd appreciate that."

"Keep in mind, Kay, that no hideaway is safe forever."

She unfolded her hands, refolded them. "If things work out exactly right, the people who most want me dead will end up defunct or incapacitated themselves, Bascom."

"You have me down as playing a part in bringing all that about?"

"Yes, you, the Cosmos Detective Agency and Jake Cardigan."

"Alicia Bower, a client of yours, already told Jake about something dubbed Surrogate 13," he said. "She pretty clearly implied that this particular sneaky Mechanix International project and the killing of my son's wife were linked."

"After Alicia left here for DC," continued the blonde attorney, "I did some more digging. Poking into things that are probably not any of my business is one of my few faults, Bascom. I found out more about what seems to be going on."

"Found out enough to get yourself turned into a target."

Nodding again, she told him what she knew.

25

THE RENTED SKYCAR told Gomez, "Impossible, *señor.*"

The detective, alone, was flying through the hot humid Managua midday. *"Ay,* it's not bad enough that the aircirc system in this clunk is considerably deficient," he mentioned to the control panel as he yet again wiped his perspiring forehead, "but now you inform me that I'm going to have vidcommercials inflicted on me for as long as I'm airborne."

"Sí, that's true."

A rectangular vidscreen filled the entire righthand side of the windshield. At the moment an impressive shot of a smoldering volcano was showing on the screen. Two voxboxes, slightly out of sync, were saying, "The Hermanos Mezclar offer you the absolute *best* volcano tour that can be obtained in all of Nicaragua. Once you sign up, which you can do, *amigos,* at any of Managua's hotels, you're guaranteed seeing not only every one of the country's eight *active* volcanoes but ten—yes, *ten* of its extinct volcanoes as well. Nothing equals—"

"Can we at least modify the volume?" inquired Gomez.

"It is at its *lowest* level now, señor."

"Eh? I can't hear you over the huckstering."

After a few seconds the control voice decided, "The *señor* is making a jest."

Gomez made a rude noise and consulted the small destination screen. According to that, he'd almost reached the Avenida Socuanjoche. He punched out a landing pattern, then leaned back in his seat and looked elsewhere than at the adscreen.

". . . in addition to the majestic Masaya volcano, you'll also behold the fiery wonders of Nindiri and San Pedro, two of—"

"I'd truly like to arrange some fiery wonders for the *hombres* who rented me this heap," observed Gomez.

With considerable shivering and rattling, the skycar settled into a landing slot in the parking area at the rear of the Club Soñador.

Quickly disembarking, Gomez stood out in the steamy day and scanned the club. It was a low L-shaped structure of imitation adobe and plastile. A large off-kilter sign up on the slanting red roof proclaimed in dusty neon letters—CLUB SOÑADOR! THE BEST IN LEGAL ILLUSIONS!

Wiping his forehead once again, Gomez crossed the buckled lot, which held five other skycars and twice that many landcars.

The rusty metal door whined forlornly as he pushed it open.

The foyer was shadowy and damp, just slightly cooler than the day outside. There was a strong smell of spices all around.

Leaning in the only other doorway was a thin young woman of twenty. Darkskinned with silvery blonde hair, she was wearing a black singlet, black trousers and boots and a narrow silver belt. "What sort of illusions are you interested in, *guapo?*" she inquired. "We can offer you holographic sex, simulated brainstim, which compares favorably with Tek yet is completely legal, or—"

"Actually, *cara,* I'm pursuing grim reality," he informed her. "Where can I find the proprietor, Dreamer Garcia?"

Smiling, she tapped herself between the breasts with her right thumb. "That's me," she said. "I'm Dreamer Garcia."

"Not unless you changed sexes and dropped twenty years since last week," he contested. "Now, *por favor,* I'd like to talk to the *true* Dreamer."

"We'll step into the office to discuss this."

A copperplated lazgun was in her left hand.

"I guess we will," agreed Gomez.

THE PRESIDENT OF the United States was not feeling at all well. Warren Brookmeyer, his dark face touched with perspiration, was crouched in the middle of the small grey room, fists clenched at his sides. "Goddamn it," he shouted. "Send somebody in here! Send someone in here at once!"

After nearly a full minute the voxbox in the low metal ceiling said, "Lie down on your cot, Mr. President. Otherwise you'll be sedated again."

"That's another damn thing I want to complain about." Brookmeyer scowled up at the overhead speaker. "I'm not supposed to be sleeping on a lousy cot. For Christ sake, I'm the president of this whole damned country. I'm Commander in Chief. I was promised a suite at this rehab center."

"Lie down on your cot," repeated the voxbox. "If you don't comply, sir, a pacifying gas will be introduced into the room."

"Not that stuff again." President Brookmeyer went and sat on the edge of the metal cot, which was the room's only piece of furniture. "The last time you bastards used that crap on me, I woke up with one hell of a hangover. Listen, I want to discuss this whole mess with the director. I demand to talk to Dr. Marchitelli. I haven't seen him once in the—what is it? In the three days I've been here."

"Dr. Marchitelli is no longer on our staff, Mr. President. Now, please, lie down. You have thirty seconds to cooperate."

Muttering, the president stretched out on the narrow cot. He lay with his arms stiff at his sides, fists clenched, and the thin pillow under his head. "I want to see whoever's in charge now, whichever doctor is supposed to be looking after me. That's a presidential order."

Part of the far wall slid away. "Which is part of the problem, Warren." Vice President McCracklin stepped into the room.

"Jim!" The president sat up. "Can you explain to me what in the hell is going on?"

"Sure, that's why I'm here, Warren." He smiled as the grey wall closed behind him.

Brookmeyer started to stand up. "Okay, first off tell me why they—"

"Stay on your cot," suggested McCracklin.

"Why the hell are you—"

"Stay there." Hands in trouser pockets, he leaned against the metal wall. "I hear you've been making a lot of fuss, Warren."

"You're damn right I have," agreed the angry president. "I came here voluntarily, Jim, as you well know. Admittedly I have a problem, but I don't think—"

"More than a problem," cut in the vice president. "You're a hopeless Tek addict. You've been doing two, three hours of the damn stuff *every* day."

"I'm not really arguing that part of it." His frown deepened as he stared, perplexed at the blond younger man. "That's the reason I'm here, Jim."

"Well, not exactly."

"What do you mean?"

McCracklin smiled slowly. "The original plan has been somewhat modified."

President Brookmeyer stood up. "Who gave you the authority to modify my plan?"

"Sit down."

Brookmeyer sat. "The plan, as you damn well know, was for me to spend a couple of weeks here to get rid of my Tek habituation." He watched the other man. "We had Mechanix International construct us that foolproof android simulacrum, which is filling in for me while I—"

"Thereby perpetrating a fraud on the American people."

"That's not what you said when we first cooked up this idea, Jim."

"Possibly, Warren, I wasn't completely truthful with you."

"But, listen, no permanent harm'll be done," Brookmeyer insisted. "Once I'm off Tek—or at least get my preoccupation under control—then I'll be back to run this country as well as ever. You know I—"

"Oh, there's not going to be any need for that."

"What are you talking about?" He left the cot.

"Sit down again." There was a stungun in Vice President McCracklin's hand.

President Brookmeyer returned to the metal bed and Mc-Cracklin explained to him what the real situation was.

26

THE THIN, PALE man turned away from Jake. "We weren't actually *friends* back in Greater Los Angeles," he said, gazing out the wide viewwindow of his living room at the hazy green of the walled courtyard garden. "In fact, we were little more than *casual* acquaintances."

Jake was sitting in a highback wicker chair, legs straight out in front of him, hands in his pockets. "I'm not," he explained, "in Nicaragua looking up old pals, Mat."

"There's another proof that we were never close. My *real* friends, Jake, all call me Matson," pointed out Matson Tabor. "Anyone who *actually* knows me, or knew me, would never address me as Mat."

"While you were teaching at SoCal Tech, you were Mat." Jake grinned. "You seem a lot more uneasy than you used to be, Matson."

"Nicaragua isn't Greater LA." He frowned over his shoulder at Jake. "I really can't afford to have it known I was interviewed by a cop from—"

"Private investigator," corrected Jake.

"It doesn't matter. The university is *very* conservative when it comes to—"

"You teach at the same college as Dr. Izabel Morgana, don't you?"

Tabor faced him. "I won't discuss Izabel with you," he said, eyeing the ceiling. "You'd better just get—"

"Relax, Matson. None of the surveillance gear is function-ing."

"What? My god, they'll think that I—"

"Nope, they'll think it was a malfunction. I rigged things that way before I arrived at your doorstep," explained Jake. "When I leave, I'll fix it back the—"

"I think you'd better leave right now."

"I have pretty thorough itineraries, put together by the Cos-mos Detective Agency, for both Arnold Maxfield, Jr. and Eve Bascom during their stay here," Jake continued. "When I was going over them, I noticed that both Junior and Eve visited you twice. Once for dinner with you and—"

"It doesn't matter *who* he was."

"And then, the day before Junior was killed, he and Eve at-tended a small cocktail party you gave. Another of your guests that night was Dr. Morgana."

"Izabel and I aren't *close* friends either," said Tabor. "But it's important that I ask certain faculty people over now and—"

"Ever hear of Surrogate 13?"

"No."

"Curious about what it might be?"

"Not in the least. Now, *please,* you have to leave."

"Anything unusual take place at your party?"

"Did Arnie tell me he expected to die a violent death the next day, do you mean?" He shook his head. "It was just another dull party. Were you *tailed* here? I don't want them to know that—"

"I ditched all my tags within five minutes of the hotel," he as-sured the uneasy professor. "What about Dr. Morgana and Eve? Did they—"

"Listen, Jake, I'll give you something." Tabor took a few steps in his direction. "But then, *really,* you have to get the hell out of my house. I can't, you know, teach in the States anymore. This position is *important* to me."

"Give me what?"

"Information," he said. "You're probably aware that Arnie

was the sort of man who wasn't satisfied with one affair at a time. He was involved not only with Eve but with Izabel."

"That I already know."

"You probably don't know, however, that Izabel was having him watched. She wanted to find out what he and Eve did and who else he might be seeing down here."

"Who did the watching, the National Security Police?"

"No, no, Izabel rarely utilized her government connections for private matters," Tabor told him. "She hired a small local outfit called Observación Discreto, run by a scoundrel named Cleve Shannon, who—"

"Used to be a private cop in Chicago."

"Is he another of your old chums?"

"Never met the guy, but his reputation was fragrant enough to have reached me in GLA," answered Jake. "He was tagging Junior during his final days, huh?"

"Shannon's *very* good at gathering dirt," said Tabor. "He's supposed to turn over *all* the material he gathers to his client, but I've heard he sometimes keeps copies."

"Meaning he might have something hidden away that's worth looking at?"

"Up to and including the fatal accident, yes."

Jake nodded, got to his feet. "Thanks, Matson," he said. "It's been terrific renewing our old friendship."

A SKEPTICAL EXPRESSION touched Gomez's face. "Are you certain, *chiquita,* that you're capable of differentiating betwixt truth and crapola?" he inquired.

The dark-clad silver blonde said, *"Papa grande,* I'm telling you the absolute truth. I—"

"If you think I'm in the grandpappy class, your perceptions obviously aren't—"

"You're twice my age, *cholo,"* she pointed out. "Now can we get back to business?"

They were in the musty office of the Club Soñador and three of the four walls were thick with foot-square monitor screens. The two dozen monitors behind the young woman's desk showed what was going on in the various holographic sex cribs on the next level down. It made a kaleidoscopic blur of real and simulated naked flesh.

"Are you offering to sell me Dreamer's current address?"

She gave him a disappointed frown. "I really am Dreamer's kid sister. My name is Rita," she said. "I've heard of you, Señor Gomez—and even more of your illustrious partner, Jake Cardigan. I think maybe you can help me *and* do yourself some good."

"How so, *cara?*" The detective was sitting on an armchair that faced her desk. "And, to keep the record straight, I happen to be every bit as illustrious as Jake. In fact, in certain circles they'd rank me higher than—"

"Can you shut your *boca* for just a moment, so I can explain?" asked Rita. "My brother disappeared yesterday, early in the morning, we think. It was, we're certain, Dacobra's men who got him. Do you know who Captain Dacobra is?"

"*Sí,* but why would his security goons grab Dreamer?"

"It could be for any number of reasons," she said. "For one thing, our esteemed government has long suspected my brother of being sympathetic to the underground Revolución Party."

"And is he?"

"In more ways than they even suspect."

"My notion is that they hauled him in for a different reason," Gomez said. "See, *cara,* it was Charley Charla up in Manhattan who—"

"*Una víbora.*"

"A dead viper."

"Charla's dead?"

Nodding, Gomez replied, "Diced by some lads with lazrifles. Quite probably because he was in the midst of providing me with information."

"What's the connection with my brother?"

"Among Charley's last words was a message to me to contact Dreamer Garcia of this address," Gomez explained. "According to Charley, your missing *hermoso* has some useful knowledge to sell me."

"About what, Gomez?"

"A connection between the Joaquim Tek Cartel and the murders of Eve Bascom and Arnold Maxfield, Junior."

"Mierda!" Rita made a rapid sign of the cross. "If those Joaquim *pendejos* are involved, then—"

"Didn't you know about any of this?"

"I know that my brother, even though he's not an especially law-abiding citizen, is strongly opposed to Tek," she answered. "He's had run-ins with Joaquim's people before. But I'm not aware of anything recent."

"The cartel is in a position to tell Captain Dacobra what to do?"

The young woman laughed. "Tek runs Nicaragua, Gomez."

Resting his elbow on the chair arm, he rested his head against his palm. "Whatever Dreamer had to sell me in the way of information was worth a thousand bucks."

"Charla could just have been lying, you know."

"No, the fact Charley's dead and Dreamer is missing seems to me to confirm the value of the tip."

"Dreamer still thinks of me most of the time as a schoolgirl." Shaking her head, she sighed. "He doesn't confide in me as much as he should."

"Okay, then we'll have to find him," said Gomez, straightening up. "So I can ask him firsthand."

"There may be a way to do that," Rita said. "Just an hour ago I was contacted by a friend of Professor Ignacio Mentosa. I don't know if you've heard of him in your country, Gomez, but he's a very important and courageous critic of the ruling junta."

"I know who Mentosa is. Matter of fact, we encountered him in the lobby of our hotel only yesterday."

"Professor Mentosa wants to meet me at nightfall," she told him. "He has news about Dreamer and how we can reach him."

"You trust Mentosa?"

"He's one of the few people in this country I do trust completely," she answered. "Can you come with me?"

Gomez said, "I can."

27

◻

BEFORE HE HIT Cleve Shannon's office, Jake stopped at the Club 900 on the Carretera Sur. The late afternoon sky had clouded over and a misty haze was settling over the city. The club's facade stretched across nearly half a block and was a gaudy patchwork of litesigns and neon tubing. *The DIRTY TALK One-Stop!* blinked one huge sign in glaring scarlet. *Talk FILTH with the Most BEAUTIFUL Holomodels in the World! Cheer An ORGY! Have A Lusty DYKE Listen To Your CONFESSION! Talk As DIRTY As You Want!*

The huge, goldplated robot doorman sneered down at Jake. "You ought to be able to do better than this, *pobrecito.*"

Jake feigned a rueful expression. "I know and it often gives me pause," he admitted. "How much?"

"Fifteen hundred *cordobas* admission fee, which includes a generous tip for me."

"Of course." Jake handed him a packet of Nicaraguan money chits. "Where might I find Daphne Dynamite? She was recommended to me as being—"

"Geez, I wouldn't have pegged you as enjoying that sort of thing." Grabbing the money, the big robot thrust it into a slot in his side. "I'd have guessed you were a straight wanker."

"Are you this critical of all the Club 900 patrons?"

The mechanical doorman made a chuckling noise. "Sure, sap. It makes you doinks feel extra guilty." He tapped the side of his golden skull with a golden forefinger, producing a rich echoing bong. "Psychology, you see, plays an important part in sex, even this paper moon kind."

"You're absolutely right. Now where do I find Daphne?"

"They'll tell you inside, rube." Behind him a wide black door slid silently out of the way. "Trot on in and enjoy yourself. And that's all you're really going to enjoy, chum, since everything else is fake."

"Hiya, *guapo,*" greeted the naked Chinese hatcheck girl. "Check your lid, please."

Jake moved across the blackwalled foyer. "Not wearing a hat, miss."

"Makes no difference, still costs you a hundred *cordobas.*"

As he paid the android, Jake said, "It's been suggested I'd enjoy Daphne Dynamite."

She looked him up and down. "You might at that," she commented. "Though you looked more like a keyhole man when I first saw you."

"Maybe later. Where do I find Daphne?"

"Use Door 14 over that way. Enjoy."

He found another robot, goldplated and jewel-encrusted, guarding the door marked DAPHNE DYNAMITE. "How much time you want with this dominating little lady?"

"Oh, fifteen minutes ought to do."

"That'll be a thousand *cordobas,* including gratuities." He held out a golden hand, palm up.

Jake gave him the money.

"And one hundred more for the coins that activate her holostage."

Jake paid that.

The room beyond the door was a shade over closet-size. There was an uncomfortable metal chair and a dirt-smeared holoplatform.

Squatting next to the coinbox, Jake took the special coin he'd brought with him out of an inner jacket pocket. He inserted it into the slot and stood back.

The room made a series of low, odd noises and the lights dimmed for roughly ten seconds.

Then a life-size projection of a plump middleaged woman arrived on the small circular stage. "I'm nowhere near as cute as Daphne Dynamite," she said.

"Matter of opinion. Did Timecheck fill you in?"

"Yes. How is he?"

"Running about four seconds slow last time I saw him." He sat on the chair. "This is completely secure?"

"Don't worry, Cardigan. I've had secret meetings here before. There's no danger of being overheard, although your reputation may suffer if you're seen coming out of here."

"It's about as low as it can sink already. You're Santilla Soledad, huh?"

"I am, *sí.*"

"Timecheck recommends you as a good source for information about the doings of the US Embassy in town."

"That's one of my specialties," she acknowledged. "I worked there for nearly three years."

"I'm interested in Dominic Hersh."

"A real *hijo de puta.*"

"That I already know," Jake said. "I'm interested in his recent activities. Particularly in relation to the late Arnold Maxfield, Jr."

"Hersh is really with the Office of Clandestine Operations. They planted him in the embassy and everybody there's aware of the fact," Santilla told him. "Hersh is more than that, though. He's also very thick with the Joaquim Tek Cartel."

"That's not exactly news to me." Jake leaned forward in the rickety chair. "Here's what I have to find out about, Santilla. First off, I want to know the names of all the people involved in the death of Eve Bascom. Then I need more information on Surrogate 13."

"I don't have the names, but I can find them," she said. "Surrogate 13 is an android dupe of the President of the United States. It was, very quietly, delivered to the embassy here about two weeks ago."

"Why here?"

"This was the staging area, Cardigan. Hersh played an important part in the operation and the final testing of the simulacrum was done here under his supervision."

"Is the andy still in town?"

She gave a negative shake of her head. "It was shipped out days ago."

"To where?"

"I hear Florida."

"Why there?"

"That's where it was to take over for the real Warren Brookmeyer."

Jake frowned. "Who's idea was all this?"

"The president himself. He's a Tekhead, you know," she continued. "The idea, as I understand it, was to use this very convincing Mechanix sim to carry on for him for a few weeks while he goes some place to try a cure for his addiction."

Jake stood, shaking his head. "Nope, that's not what's going on," he said toward the projection. "You don't kill people simply to keep them from revealing a con."

Santilla smiled. "Ah, I forgot for a moment that you're an American," she said. "To me covering up something like this with a few murders seems perfectly logical. They killed my father five years ago for something much less important."

"Something's being covered up, Santilla, but I think it's more than just using an android double for Brookmeyer."

She offered, "I can suggest someone else you ought to talk to. Keep in mind, however, that she's a civilian. That is, not a revolutionary or an informant."

"Who we talking about?"

"Her name is Gabrielle Kastle. She works for the Nicaraguan office of MaxComm and until a week ago was romantically involved with Dominic Hersh."

"He doesn't sound like a guy anybody'd want to get romantically tangled up with."

"I said exactly that to Gabrielle more than once."

"So she's a friend of yours?"

She nodded. "Do you want me to try to arrange a meeting?"

"Sure, but someplace other than here."

"Don't worry. Gabrielle would never—even holograph-ically—enter a place like this. I'll contact you soon as I can, Cardigan."

As he said, *"Gracias,"* she faded from the room.

28

◨

JAKE GOT THREE separate views of the second killing. Three intensely sharp and bright monitor screens showed him the murder from assorted angles.

He was down in the basement Security Room of the office building that housed the Observación Discreto detective agency up on Level 3. Jake had used his breaking and entering skills to gain him admission to the area just three minutes ago.

He'd planned to use a stungun on the human guard who watched over the building's hundred-plus watchdog screens. Then he'd go up and try to persuade Shannon to share his files on Junior Maxfield and Eve Bascom with him. Jake didn't want anyone with the capability of calling in the law to witness that discussion.

A fair plan, except somebody else had been here first.

The guard, his right hand just inches from the alarm toggle, was slumped down in his chair. Nearly half of the top of his skull was gone, sliced away by the beam of a lazgun.

While Jake was standing there, a couple feet behind the dead man, he checked the trio of screens that provided a view of the inside of Cleve Shannon's office.

"Jesus!"

Two men wearing the now-familiar plastiglass face masks and crimson berets had come busting into the hefty operative's room.

Jake slapped the sound key.

". . . the hell do you clowns think you're doing?"

Neither of the Red Angels said a word.

"Captain Dacobra and I are," Shannon started to tell them.

But then the shimmering beam of the first lazgun hit him. It severed the hand that had been inching toward the lazgun sitting next to the vidphone.

Jake got to see that from three different points of view, heard the detective scream with pain.

The second lazgun crackled, then the first one again. Shannon roared once more before he was cut clean in two. Blood exploded, masking one of the security camera lenses.

Exhaling, Jake took a backward step.

Then he heard a woman cry out in pain. A third Red Angel appeared in the office doorway. He was holding a woman in front of him. He had her right arm twisted behind her back and his other hand clutching her throat.

It was a slender blonde woman of forty.

"Bev Kendricks," said Jake, recognizing the private investigator.

Pivoting, he ran from the room.

THE LAKESIDE HOUSE was called the Villa Flor and once, long ago, it had been surrounded by formal gardens. After the severe earthquakes of thirty years back, when the private chapel and one entire wing of the villa had collapsed, the plants and flowers had been left to grow wild. Now in the rainy twilight outside the living room you saw a sprawling tangle of yellow and scarlet blossoms, of twisty, thorny vines and giant shaggy shrubs with jagged mounds of smashed brick and stone rising up out of it.

Gomez, seated alone on a long low sofa, was scanning the sea of foliage out there in the gathering darkness. So far he'd spotted two armed guards. One, a hefty young woman with a lazrifle, was hunkered against the remains of the chapel's bell tower.

Gomez and Rita, who was occupying a rattan armchair, had arrived more than ten minutes ago for their meeting with Professor Mentosa.

But he hadn't as yet appeared and, except for a large bearded youth who stood with arms folded in the arched doorway, they were alone in the big vaulted living room.

"You seem," observed Rita, "uneasy, Gomez."

"I'm merely reflecting, *bonita*," he told her. "Wondering if, despite the infinite wisdom stored in my capable *cabeza*, I've come toddling into a trap."

"Do you think I'd set you up?"

"Might be the prof is the one who—"

"This isn't a trap, Señor Gomez." The short greyhaired man he'd seen attacked in the hotel lobby came into the room now. Mentosa was in a robot wheelchair. "Allow me, by the way, to thank you. I've been told that you scared off my attackers after I was stungunned."

Gomez held up a correcting finger. "Actually that was my partner, Jake Cardigan," he said. "He's quicker on the trigger than I am."

"Convey him my gratitude. I would have been killed if someone hadn't taken action quickly." The chromed chair whirred him to the center of the room. "I've heard many good things about the both of you. An old and trusted friend of mine in Mexico, who's fighting a very successful battle against the oppressors, speaks very highly of you."

"Would that be Warbride?"

"*Sí.*" He rolled over to Rita, held out both hands. "How are you, *paloma?*"

"I'm very worried about my brother, Professor," she answered, taking hold of his hands. "You know something about what happened to him, don't you?"

Mentosa gave a sad shake of his head. "The news is not good," he said. "Yet I feel there's hope."

"Where is he?"

Looking out into the wild garden, the greyhaired professor answered, "They've taken him, along with several other suspected rebels, to the Isla Chanza Detention Station."

"*Dios!*" She let go his hands and pressed hers to her heart. "How can you say there's any hope?"

"What's this Isla Chanza set up?" asked Gomez.

"Nobody comes back from there." Rita started to cry softly. "Nobody, never."

"That's not true, child." The professor's chair took him nearer to Gomez. "There is a manmade island out there in Lake Managua." He gestured at the rainy night. "Political prisoners are detained in a prison facility there, processed and—"

"Tortured," said Rita quietly, sobbing. "Tortured, maimed. They'll do terrible things to Dreamer and then—"

"Easy, child," said Professor Mentosa. "Many prisoners actually do leave the island, Señor Gomez. The problem, however, is that they leave there for much worse federal prisons or for the Termination Station on the outskirts of our city of Granada."

"Where," inquired the detective, "does the hope come in?"

"There are," answered Professor Mentosa, "several people being held on the island that we want to see freed."

Rita popped to her feet. "Wait—you're not going to try a raid? That's impossible," she told him, voice rising. "Everybody'll get killed and so will Dreamer in the process."

The professor said calmly, "Child, unless something is done, very soon, your brother and many another will almost certainly die anyway."

"Yes, I know that, but—"

"Calm down," Gomez advised her. "The professor apparently has a plan worked out."

Sitting back down, but on the edge of the chair, the young woman said, "It won't succeed. People have tried to spring prisoners from Isla Chanza before. Every damned one failed."

Gomez nodded at the man in the wheelchair. "How are you going to work it?" he asked. "And, more important, how are you intending to avoid ending up dead?"

"I'll explain," said Mentosa.

29

THERE WAS A Red Angel on the second level of the building. Jake, coming up carefully from below and staying in the shadows at the ramp edge, spotted the lookout before he was spotted himself.

Easing out his stungun, Jake aimed and fired.

The man at the top of the ramp made a surprised gasping sound, muffled by his plastiglass mask, as the stunbeam jabbed into his midsection.

He took one jerking step backward, elbows snapping against his sides; his lazgun dropped from his gloved hand and started to slide down the steep ramp. He tumbled over onto his knees, went lurching over and began sliding down in the wake of the weapon.

Already moving, Jake grabbed up the skidding gun. He took hold of the unconscious Red Angel and propped him roughly against the wall.

"I'll just," he said quietly, "borrow a few things from you."

BEV KENDRICKS SAID, "You fellows aren't being smart."

"Shut up, *puta,*" advised one of the masked Red Angels.

"I'm an American investigator," she told them, rubbing at the fresh bruise on her cheek. "Treating me badly is going to cause a stewpot of trouble for—"

"He was a *gringo,* too." The other masked man, taller and

broader than his colleague, jerked a thumb in the direction of the bloody remains of Cleve Shannon. "That didn't do him a hell of a lot of good, *señorita.* Now, *por favor,* tell me why you came here."

"I already did," said the blonde detective. "I'm in Managua working on a case for an American client. I dropped in on Shannon to see if I could hire him to help on some local angles in the—"

"Quit the *mierda.*" The large Red Angel slapped her, hard, across the face again. "Your client happens to be Arnold Maxfield, Sr. He would never authorize your employing of a *cabrón* like Shannon." He kicked at the part of the dead man that lay on the floor near his booted foot.

"Trouble!" announced Jake from the doorway. He was wearing the borrowed crimson beret and the darktinted face mask.

"What is it, Carlito?" asked the one who was questioning Bev.

"Cardigan is downstairs."

The other man laughed. "That *mariposa* won't make any trouble," he said. "Rudy, you and Carlito go down and take care of the bastard."

"I think you're underestimating him," said Jake. Bringing up his right hand, he fired his stungun at the bigger man.

While the large man was making a gagging sound, one hand clawing at this mask, Jake spun and shot the remaining Red Angel.

Both men hit the floor hard, sending blood splashing up.

Jake tilted the mask up off his face. "Nice running into you again, Bev," he said, grinning.

"JUST TRUST ME, okay?" said the blonde, putting both hands against the edge of the dead detective's heavy desk. "Help me shove this damned thing aside."

"There's a safe under there?" inquired Jake, joining her in shoving. "You're sure about—"

"C'mon, Jake. I had a headstart on this end of things, remember?"

The desk moved, skidding and wobbling some when it hit a thick spill of blood.

"Are we," inquired Jake as Bev dropped to her knees, "going to share this cache of information?"

"Hush a minute, you're distracting me." Head low, she was scanning the plaztile squares that covered the floor where the big desk had been. Yanking a plyochief out of a pocket of her tan slax, she wiped away a splatter of blood and bile. "This one." She tapped the square she'd just scrubbed, then frowned up at him. "Yeah, I suppose I'll have to share whatever's here with you, since you, more or less, saved my life just now."

"More or less? Hey, those louts were about one step from—"

"I had a contingency plan. I was just about to use it when you came barging in."

"Oh, so? What the hell was it? Looked to me like—"

"I may want to use it against you sometime." Resting on her haunches, she glanced around the office. "We need Shannon's right hand now."

"It's a print recog safe?"

"Obviously." Bev rose up, frowning around at the scattered sections of the detective's body. "Nope, that's his left hand there next to Rudy."

"You know, I've been carrying around this image in my head of a sweet, demure detective," remarked Jake. "But now I'm wondering if I—"

"Bullshit," she countered. "I was tough when we were both cops years ago in Greater LA, Jake. I'm, if anything, even tougher now that I'm on my own." She located the right arm and grabbed it up. Crouching, she slapped the dead detective's right-hand palm down on the designated square of tiling.

She ran her tongue over her lower lip, concentrating, as she adjusted the placing of the dead fingers on the square that served as the hidden cover for the safe.

"Some of these gadgets also require body heat," mentioned Jake.

"Not this one." She placed her own hand over the dead one and pressed down hard.

After ten seconds came two metallic clicks and then a low whirring hum.

The square of tile slid aside to reveal a deep open storage bin below, packed with vidcassettes, audiobytes and bundles of papers.

"Get rid of this chunk of Shannon, so I can dig out what we need," requested Bev, giving the dead hand a shove.

"Yes, ma'am." He took care of the job. "How'd you find out about Shannon and what he was up to?"

"The same damn way, I imagine, that you did, from an informant," she answered. "I've got a secure hangout where we can go to look over this stuff. You can come with me or you can go to hell—I won't come anywhere near a Cosmos setup."

Jake grinned. "I accept your invitation."

30

BEV TOUCHED THE control pad and the wallscreen abruptly quit showing them the naked images of Eve Bascom and Arnold Maxfield, Jr. "What's the matter?" she asked.

The light in the small techroom came up slowly.

Blinking, Jake asked, "Why'd you stop?"

"You made a sound. Sounded like you were in pain."

He was sitting in a black metal chair, a few feet from her. "Sorry, I didn't realize I'd said anything out loud. Go on, let's see the rest of this sequence."

The infocomp system Bev was using had assimilated all the material they'd taken away from the private detective's file of dupe surveillance material. After swiftly scanning and sorting it all, the system had pulled all the vid footage that contained any mention of the Surrogate 13 project.

Jake and the blonde detective had been watching footage of the couple in the communications heir's hotel suite in Managua for the past ten minutes or so. Apparently they'd done quite a bit of their talking while in bed.

"They're both dead and gone," said Bev. "Is that what's unsettling you?"

"Seeing them making love." He shook his head. "Seems like that's something nobody else ought to be watching."

Leaving her chair, she moved to his side. "When you're betrayed, sometimes it's better just to imagine what went on," Bev said quietly. "Actually seeing what happened, the specifics of everything—that can be rough."

"I didn't know Eve Bascom, never even met her," he said. "She was dead before we—"

"I was thinking of your wife."

After a few seconds Jake said, "I guess I was, too."

"That's all over and done with."

"Yeah, and the people my onetime wife and I used to be— we're as dead as Eve Bascom and her lover."

Bev squeezed his shoulder, then returned to her chair. "We're getting some useful stuff," she said. "Want to continue?"

Jake nodded. "Yeah," he said. "I promise, no more outbursts."

CAPTAIN DACOBRA PUT on his pants. He'd left them, neatly folded, on the fat pink armchair nearest the wide oval bed. Barefoot and shirtless, he crossed to the one-way viewindow and gazed out into the rainy night. The lights of the city below were blurred and seemed to blend together to make huge abstract smears of color across the blackness. "I have some bad news about your lover," he said.

"Which one?" Izabel Morgana was sitting, naked, on the far edge of her bed.

Smiling, Dacobra returned to the pink chair to reclaim his neosilk shirt. "Forgive me, I should have been more specific," he said as he began putting on the shirt. "I mean Dominic Hersh."

A thin, dark woman with shortcut black hair, Izabel shrugged her bare shoulders. "Someone wants him dead?"

"I'm afraid so."

"Who suggested this?"

"Our friend to the North, Vice President McCracklin," replied the captain of the security police.

"Poor Dominic." Izabel stood, slowly, up. "He's been assuming that, since he betrayed President Brookmeyer, he'd made himself wealthy for life."

"He did," said Dacobra. "What he didn't anticipate was that his life would end tonight."

"Has it already been set in motion?" She walked toward the partially open doorway of her pink bathroom.

Dacobra nodded. "One more loose end taken care of, *cara.*"

Izabel stopped in the doorway, framed by pale pink light. "I want Jake Cardigan dead," she said, her left hand resting on the doorjamb. "Along with Sid Gomez and that Kendricks bitch."

"Gomez's death is, as you know, in the works," he reminded.

"You should have been able to get rid of both Cardigan and that woman at Shannon's office this afternoon."

"Izabel, I don't control the *Angeles Rojos* as completely as you seem to think," he told her. "Sometimes they go astray and botch a job." He seated himself on the fat chair, began pulling on one sock. "Keep in mind that Gomez will be dead before morning. You'll have to settle for that for the moment."

SHOULDERS HUNCHED, EYES nearly shut, Walt Bascom was standing in the middle of his tower office in the Cosmos Detective Agency building and playing his saxophone. The lights were down low and he was working on his version of a twentieth-century bop tune titled "Perdido."

The overhead voxbox broke in to inform him, "Cardigan on Holostage 1, chief."

The agency boss's eyes snapped open and he ceased tootling. "Great, put him on." He crossed to his desk, tossed the sax down atop the sprawl of clutter.

Jake, straddling a straight chair, materialized on the platform. "Still in the office, huh?"

"Been trying to get hold of you. I have . . . You're looking exceptionally glum, Jake. Something wrong?"

"No, must be the transmission," Jake assured him. "Before I report what I know, tell me why you've been trying to reach me."

Bascom dragged a wingchair over closer to the holostage. "I was contacted by Kay Norwood, your pal Alicia's lawyer chum—and, I might add, a handsome lady indeed," he commenced. "Before I assisted her in scramming to a place of relative safety, she passed on some information that pertains to the whole Surrogate 13 mess."

"That's why Eve was killed," Jake said, shaking his head. "Certain bastards were afraid she knew what was going on. She didn't actually, but it was simpler just to kill her and not take chances."

"No, she didn't even know much about the original plan," said Bascom. "That involved substituting an android ringer for that buffoon President Brookmeyer."

"Yeah, so he could sign himself up for a Tek cure and not be missed while undergoing the treatment."

"Typical halfassed government duplicity and flimflam," observed the agency chief.

"Unfortunately Junior Maxfield got wind of that original switch plan, which was being staged out of the American Embassy in Nicaragua," said Jake. "A diplomat-OCO agent name of Dominic Hersh was running that, with the cooperation of several local thugs. Maxfield got the notion he could finance his independent communications operation with dough extorted from Hersh and other officials."

"Stupid yunk. That's what got him killed," said Bascom, scowling. "He's no loss, but Eve . . ."

"There are vidtapes of the two of them together, Walt," said Jake, his voice low. "He confided in her some of what he found out and what he was planning. That's how the others found out."

"There's no need for my son to see any of that footage."

"He won't," said Jake. "Maxfield and Eve were killed to keep them from talking about Surrogate 13. But, as I see it, that was because somebody worked out a variation on the original plan. That second plan is the dangerous one."

"That's what I figure, too," Bascom told him. "Whoever's behind it isn't going to let the real Brookmeyer come back from his cure. They're going to run the country from here on out with the sim."

"That could be very lucrative," said Jake. "The biggest Tek cartel down here is tangled in this as well. They must figure an android Brookmeyer will be more sympathetic to their point of view."

"Okay, there's a lady down there in Managua who can give you a lot more details," said the chief. "I got her name from Kay Norwood. She was cozy with this Hersh schmuck and now she's lying low for fear of—"

"Gabrielle Kastle?"

"The same. Have you talked to her already?"

"Nope, I haven't been able to track her down yet. Got people working on it."

"I know where she's hiding out." Bascom gave him an address and a password. "Get to her quick, find out what she knows and then help her get the hell out of Nicaragua intact."

"How's Richard doing?"

"Growing up, which can be painful as hell. He trusted that woman and . . ." Bascom didn't finish his sentence.

"Don't blush, Walt. I see the parallel between your son's faith in his wife and mine in Kate," said Jake. "You can talk about stuff like that to me now and I won't scream, yell or swoon."

"Sorry. What about Gomez—what's he up to?"

"He's tracking down an informant named Dreamer Garcia."

Bascom said, "Both of you lads take care of yourselves."

"You're sounding almost paternal."

"Ignore it," advised Bascom. "I'm not myself lately."

31

◻

DOMINIC HERSH HAD been an exceptionally good boy and this picnic this afternoon was his reward.

The day couldn't have been better, all sunshine and crystal blue skies.

And the best part of it all was that his mother was going to attend the picnic.

Sitting stiff and straight in the skylimo, Hersh smiled in anticipation. He was eight days beyond his tenth birthday. His mother hadn't been at his party. That wasn't her fault, though. Hersh's father had made her go to Europe someplace.

It wasn't really fair, but his mother had asked him, please, not to make a fuss. It upset his father when he did that.

Shit, just about everything upset his father.

But the picnic was going to be great. The day was wonderful and he'd be seeing his mother any minute now.

He felt the excitement growing inside him as the gleaming silvery skylimo began its graceful descent toward the bright green fields below.

If Hersh hadn't been such a well-behaved little boy, he would have laughed out loud, bounced up and down on the deep soft seat and shouted for joy.

But, as his mother had pointed out more than once, well-mannered boys didn't do things like that. She was certain he'd always be a good boy and that it wouldn't be necessary, as it had been with his older brother, to send him to the Willingham Military Academy.

Dominic had promised her he'd always be good. She'd smiled, kissed him fleetingly on the cheek and assured him that he'd never have to go to that place.

The landing was so gentle that the boy wasn't immediately aware of it.

"Hey, kid," said Grooms, the huge android chauffeur, "get off your ox. We're there."

"I'm sorry, I was daydreaming."

"Like always."

The door whispered open.

Laughing quietly, the boy hopped politely from the vehicle.

Down the slanting green hillside, near a small shimmering pond that lay at the edge of a woodland, a bright red-and-white tablecloth had been spread neatly on the ground.

A big yellow picnic hamper sat square in the middle of the checkered cloth.

The boy laughed again as he began running. He was careful not to be clumsy, because his mother didn't like him when he was clumsy or awkward and stumbled or fell down.

He reached the bulging hamper without a mishap. He glanced over at the trees, an anticipatory smile on his face. In the shadows between the trees he saw someone standing and watching him.

"Mom?"

Twigs crackled and dry leaves rustled as the figure approached him. "She couldn't make it, Hersh," said Frank Dockert.

The boy clasped his hands together, puzzled. "You aren't supposed to be at my picnic," he protested. "I don't even know you yet."

The husky black man entered the sunlight. "This was my idea," he explained. "It appeals to me, showing up in your little Tek fantasy this way, Hersh."

The boy was afraid. "No, go away. This is *my* dream, bought and paid for," he said, angry. "I'm the only one who can program the Brainbox."

"Not true actually," Dockert said, smiling. "We jobbed your Brainbox about an hour ago—some of my boys did. Put in a very special Tek chip that's rigged to do a couple of unusual things."

"My mother's supposed to be here, not you!"

"This chip allows me to make this little appearance, Hersh, and inform you that your services are no longer needed."

"What are you talking about? I'm a good boy and . . ." He clenched his fists, shivering. "Listen, Dockert, I helped you on this whole thing, you and McCracklin. The president trusted me and that's why—"

"Exactly. Brookmeyer trusted you and you doublecrossed him. McCracklin figures, down the road apiece, you'll do the same damn thing to him."

"He knows I wouldn't do that."

"There's another thing this special chip does. It induces a fatal stroke."

"No, that's impossible."

"Not at all, Hersh. Tek junkies are suffering strokes, seizures and assorted fits all the time." Dockert smiled. "You'll be found—with an innocent chip substituted for ours—dead amidst your Tek paraphernalia."

"No! I'm not going to let you get away with this, Dockert."

"Now, now, Dominic. What have I told you about temper tantrums?" His mother, beautiful as ever, was standing next to the black man.

"Mom. Please, you won't let them hurt me."

She shook her head sadly. "It can't be helped, dear. You have to accept this like a little man."

Then she was gone.

Night suddenly closed down on the field and the woods.

Hersh's life ended.

THE DAMPNESS WAS thick all around them. You could feel it, smell it and it seemed to be waiting for the chance to take you over.

Rita Garcia edged closer to Gomez on the rear seat of the landvan. *"Malo,"* she said in a small uneasy voice.

The heavy vehicle was rolling slowly through the long, dark tunnel, its dimmed headlight beams struggling to cut into the musty blackness.

"I can understand," Gomez said to the huddled blonde, "why this isn't included on the regular scenic tour of Managua."

"Do enclosed places bother you, Señor Gomez?" Professor Mentosa asked from his seat next to the broadshouldered driver.

"Tunnels that burrow under the waters of a lake aren't my favorite spots," he admitted. "Especially tunnels that don't look as though they'd won any architectural prizes lately."

"Oh, I assure you this tunnel is perfectly safe," said the grey-haired professor. "Up until less than six months ago it was used regularly to transport supplies to the Isla Chanza facility. Then, chiefly because of some clever manipulations by a relative of General Alcazar's, a fleet of watercraft took over the job."

"Foolhardy," said Rita, taking hold of Gomez's arm.

The professor shifted in his seat so that he could look directly back at her. "This raid was planned, and all the details carefully worked out, *before* your unfortunate brother was arrested, child." He gestured at the van that was following them through the underwater tunnel. "We have sufficient personnel for this. And, more importantly, allies inside the detention station. There will be, if we're lucky, no fighting and no bloodshed. Your brother will be added to the four prisoners we were already intending to get out of here. We'll pick them up at the agreed rendezvous spot, then make our way safely back through this tunnel."

"I'm not," she told him, "feeling especially lucky."

"All will go well, you'll see, *paloma.*"

Gomez asked, "Who are the other four, Professor?"

"Political prisoners, all loyal rebels," he answered. "I'm especially eager to free Nestor Gonsalves, a respected colleague of mine."

Rita's grip on Gomez's arm tightened. "You're certain, Professor, that Gonsalves is still there?"

"Oh, yes," he answered. "We heard from him only yesterday, when he was able to smuggle a message out to us. In fact, Gonsalves is playing an important part in the inside aspect of this whole operation."

Leaning closer to Gomez, the young woman whispered in his ear. "Gonsalves was killed a week ago in Granada. I *know.*"

32

THE NIGHT RAIN hit at the landcar as it moved along the Boulevar De Los Mártires. Bev was driving.

They were passing a large park, a mixture of real and holographic trees and shrubs. The storm was causing the projectors to malfunction and a long, high hedge of flowering yellow blossoms kept vanishing and reappearing, giving intermittent glimpses of a heroic, larger-than-life-size statue of General Alcazar.

"Even larger than life," remarked Jake, "the general looks short."

"I appreciate your letting me tag along on this interview with Gabrielle Kastle," she said, guiding the car through the rainy night.

"You shared the Shannon stuff with me," he pointed out. "Besides which, we're not having a contest or a race."

"We work for rival detective agencies."

"The people who arranged the murders of Eve Bascom and Junior Maxfield will never go to trial," Jake said. "There are too many political angles, too much Tek cartel influence. What I want to do is get the whole story on what happened and why."

"And then try a little vigilante justice?"

"Depends. You're working for Maxfield, Senior," he said. "He's somebody who can get the truth out in the open."

"MaxComm doesn't always deal in the truth."

"I'll settle for a close approximation," said Jake. "I just don't want to see Brookmeyer and Hersh and Dr. Morgana and the rest of them get away clean."

She turned onto a wide side street. "I've been wanting to talk to you about the last time we encountered each other," Bev said, watching the wet night street ahead. "The whole mess with Alicia Bower."

"Over and done," he told her.

"I was working on her disappearance for the family," she said. "Much as I hate to admit it, I let people con me."

"That's because of your sweet and trusting nature."

"The point I'm getting at, if you'll quit interrupting me with smug remarks, Jake, is that I never tried to sidetrack you," Bev told him. "I gave you fake information, but, trust me, I really did think it was true at the time."

Jake nodded, grinning. "I know," he assured her.

After a moment she asked, "Are you seeing her?"

"Alicia Bower, you mean?"

"I've been hearing rumors that you and the girl are—"

"We aren't," he said. "Although she did give me some information on this case. Mechanix International, you know, whipped up Surrogate 13 while her father was still above the ground."

"She's pretty young," mentioned Bev, eyes on the wet road. "Compared to you, that is."

"True," agreed Jake. "There's the church we're looking for. Up ahead on your left."

THE LANDVAN ROLLED to a stop a few yards from a high, wide dark-metal door. Smiling amiably, Professor Mentosa looked back over his seat at Gomez and Rita. There was a coppery lazgun in his right hand. "I'd appreciate it," he told them, "if you'd both, very slowly and carefully, get out of the van now, *por favor.*"

"So much for one of the few trustworthy *hombres* in Nicaragua," remarked Gomez.

Rita said, "The *cochino* has sold out to them."

"Now, now, don't think badly of Ignacio Mentosa." The grey-haired man made a get-moving gesture with the lazgun.

"A sim," said Gomez, sliding toward the door. "I'm turning *muy inepto* in my old age. I should've spotted you a couple reels back, Prof."

"I'm a testimonial to the skill of Mechanix International."

"So you've been playing decoy, Judas goat," said Gomez.

"*Sí,* and rounding up quite a collection of traitors and enemies of the state," he said. "Go along now, move into the tunnel. *Pronto!*"

As they stepped out into the musty shadows, Rita asked, "Where's the real Mentosa?"

Chuckling, the android dupe climbed out of the halted van. He pointed a thumb at the dark ceiling. "You'll be meeting the respected gentleman very shortly," he promised. "It'll be a brief encounter."

With considerable rattling and ratcheting, the big metal door swung open. Standing in the yellow-lit corridor were ten uniformed men armed with lazrifles.

"My brother," said Rita. "Is he really here on Isla Chanza?"

"In a manner of speaking, *cara.*"

She took a step toward him. "What do you mean?"

"Dreamer, alas, managed to annoy some of the officials and . . ." The android shrugged. "You can, possibly, view his body before—"

"*Cabrón!*"

Before Gomez could stop her, the angry young woman went charging at the false Professor Mentosa.

Chuckling again, he swung out with his free hand.

The slap hit her on the chin, caused her head to jerk back and her teeth to click.

Slumping, she started to fall to the stone floor.

Gomez lunged, catching her and holding her up.

The android eyed him. "Are you going to try anything, Señor Gomez?"

"Not yet," he answered.

33

GABRIELLE KASTLE WAS a plump redhaired woman of forty. "Does this place give you the willies?" she asked them.

"Not especially," answered Jake.

"We'll get you moved somewhere less gloomy," promised Bev.

They were in one of the crypts beneath the ancient San Norberto Church. On three sides of the stonewalled room were stone shelves holding sturdy handcarved coffins. Effigies of angels, saints and warriors adorned the coffin lids.

In a cleared space near the arched doorway of the low, dusty room, a small folding table and three chairs had been set up. A celamp resting on the table provided a thin whitish light. There were a thermoflask of nearcaf and a half a soyloaf sandwich next to the lamp.

"Do you think about death much?" Gabrielle asked. "Your own death, I mean. I've never been especially morbid, yet since I've been hiding out down here, I—"

"Let's look at the more practical aspects of death," Jake cut in to suggest. "Who's trying to kill you, ma'am?"

Sighing, she reached for the thermos. "Want any nearcaf?"

"No," said Bev.

"I suppose I'm avoiding answering. It's such an unpleasant thing to talk about." She poured herself a half cup. "It was Dom. That is, he's the one who instigated—"

"You're talking about Dominic Hersh?" asked Jake.

"Yes." She glanced at Bev. "I keep picking the worst sort of men. None of them as bad as my last husband, but . . . Sorry, forgive me. Being on the run, living down here among all these dead people . . . Dom . . . Dominic Hersh, after I told him I couldn't put up with what was going on and refused to see him any longer . . . well, he apparently arranged for my death. Fortunately, I was warned in time to—"

"Suppose," said Jake, "you tell us what it is you know."

"I thought that was what I've been doing. No, I guess I'm babbling. Dom was always criticizing me for—"

"We know about Surrogate 13," said Bev.

Jake added, "But not about the switch in the original plan. Tell us how Hersh figures in that."

Gabrielle sipped at her nearcaf. "I really hate the taste of this stuff," she said. "Allright—that wasn't his idea, sabotaging President Brookmeyer's original plan. You see, McCracklin, who's a dreadful man under all that smiling—Anyway, the vice president got to Dominic. He promised all sorts of things. Including, you understand, a great deal more money than Brookmeyer ever talked about."

"They're not going to switch back from the android stand-in," said Jake. "Is that the idea?"

"Yes, exactly, Mr. Cardigan. Right now the President Brookmeyer who's doing that idiotic Cracker Barrel Express tour is the simulacrum provided by Mechanix International," she said. "Modified somewhat, so that McCracklin can control it. That android will simply replace Brookmeyer for good, meaning that McCracklin and his cronies will control the country."

Bev asked her, "What are they planning to do with the *real* Brookmeyer?"

"Well, once they're certain the android is working effectively and fooling everybody, they'll . . . President Brookmeyer simply won't leave the medical center."

"Where is he now?"

"At the Bergstrom Clinic. That's in Florida, in the Miami Enclave."

Bev stood up. "Was Hersh involved directly in the killing of Arnold Maxfield, Jr. and Eve Bascom?"

"There was a group of them who worked all that out," replied Gabrielle. "Dr. Izabel Morgana, Captain Dacobra and Dominic. There was also someone from the Joaquim Tek Cartel, but I never found out who. Once they'd decided to keep that android dupe in office, they couldn't afford to allow Maxfield and his mistress to run around alive. It was while they were planning Maxfield's death that I ended things with Dominic."

"But you didn't warn Maxfield," said Jake.

She shook her head. "No, I wasn't strong enough to do that," she admitted. "You see—My god!"

An enormous rumbling had begun beneath the stone floor.

The floor seemed to jump, great jagged cracks came crackling cross it. The walls shook and a wooden coffin leaped from a shelf to crash down on the swaying floor.

The lid cracked, popped off. A yellowed skeleton, wound in a tattered grey shroud, came rattling out of the casket and jumped toward Gabrielle. Its bony right hand brushed down across her skirt.

"Quake!" she cried, stumbling back. "Earthquake."

Jake leaped free of his swaying chair, put an arm around Bev and headed them for the doorway.

The lamp hopped, skidded and smashed on the jittery floor.

Darkness took over.

THE THICKSET GUARD saluted as Captain Dacobra came striding into the chill room.

"This is *muy triste*," the captain said, nodding in Gomez's direction. "I am most sorry."

The small green-walled room was on the second level of the Detention Station. Its windows gave a view of the choppy night waters of Lake Managua and a scattering of supply boats docked at the metal pier.

Gomez was slumped in a metal chair, his face streaked with drying blood. He got, swaying some, to his feet. "Where do I go to lodge a formal complaint, Cap?"

The captain smiled thinly. "I am truly unhappy that my men treated you in an unkindly manner, Señor Gomez."

"Unkindly? Hey, they stomped on my *cabeza* with their damned boots."

Dacobra nodded sympathetically. "Their behavior while escorting you up here from the tunnel is unforgivable," he said. "And how are you faring, Señorita Garcia?"

"Maricón!" Rita rose up from her chair, fisting her right hand and raising it high. *"Lambioso!"*

Dacobra gave her a sad look. "It is, after all, your fault that he's in this serious trouble. You ought to have realized, when you persuaded him to help on a raid of a government facility, that—"

"We can skip all this crapola," suggested Gomez. "You had your pet andy lure us into a trap. So what next?"

"The pretty *niña* is a citizen of this country and a known revolutionary. She will be executed as a traitor," the captain explained. "You, Señor Gomez, will be detained for a trial. I must warn you, however, that your chances of ever—*Dios!*"

An enormous thumping had started. The floor bounced, the windows exploded, jagged shards of plastiglass came flickering into the room along with gusts of night rain.

"Temblor!" cried Rita, gripping Gomez's arm. "It's a quake, a bad one."

The walls of the room kept shuddering. Then, amidst considerable roaring, the ceiling broke into great ragged fragments and came cascading down on them.

34

◻

J<small>AKE BECAME AWARE</small> of a pained sobbing.

He was lying flat out, surrounded by thick darkness.

When he tried a slow deep breath, he discovered there was something heavy pressing down on his back. Ragged hunks of stone were shoving into his midsection.

There was a literod in his jacket pocket. But his right arm was pinned down by what felt like a large wooden beam. His left arm felt numb, wouldn't respond to his control.

"I'm hurt," complained a weak voice nearby. "My ribs are cracked, I think."

"Gabrielle?" he tried to say. The name came out a rusty croak.

Jake remembered he'd been trying to get Bev to the protection of the heavy door archway. Then he was going back for Gabrielle Kastle.

But he hadn't accomplished that. He'd been bashed on the head.

By what?

Part of the ceiling probably, or maybe a falling coffin or a stray stone angel.

"I'm over here," said Gabrielle. "I'm under some ceiling beams, I think."

"Going to take a while to reach you," Jake told her. "I'm stuck, too. Is Bev okay? Bev?"

Light blossomed a few feet ahead of him. "I'm in pretty good shape." The blonde detective was holding a literod of her own, playing the beam along the rubble on the floor of the corridor. "You managed to push me ahead of you when part of the roof came tumbling down."

"What's it look like up ahead? Are we going to spend the rest of our days in this crypt?"

She used the light to show him. "Roof held in this passway here," she said. "And the stairway to the ground level looks safe. No way of telling what the situation is up in the church."

"Okay," said Jake, struggling again to free his right arm. "Think you can dig me out, Bev? Then we'll unearth Gabrielle and try to work our way outside."

"I wish," said Gabrielle, "you wouldn't refer to us as though we were dead and buried."

"Sorry, must be the surroundings," said Jake.

Resting the literod on a fallen wood beam, Bev said, "I didn't figure our collaboration was going to include excavation."

GOMEZ MUTTERED, *"Dios mio."*

Gingerly, not yet certain all of his inner workings were intact and functioning, he pushed against the debris-thick floor. Dust and mortar fell away from him.

Teetering, he stood up and took a look around. Most of the ceiling had come falling down, but nothing heavy had fallen directly on Gomez.

Captain Dacobra hadn't been as lucky. He was sprawled a few feet away, partially buried under great chunks of plaster and hefty fragments of plastibeams. His skull had a new shape and there was blood easing away from his broken body and mingling with the debris on the buckled floor.

Gomez squatted, spotting the barrel of the late captain's lazgun protruding from under a twist of metal rod and a tangle of shorn wiring. He carefully began to extract the weapon.

"That will do, Señor Gomez!"

The Professor Mentosa android had appeared in what was left

of the doorway. Out of his wheelchair, standing with a lazgun aimed directly at Gomez.

"Come mierda," suggested Gomez as he dropped flat out and tugged the gun completely free.

Rolling over rubble, Gomez fired twice at the andy.

The first blast went wild, but the second scored.

The sizzling beam of the gun cut across the fake Mentosa's chest. The chest exploded, spewing out wires, cogs, tiny tubes and broken circuitry, all mixing with shreds of his shirt and jacket.

"Bueno." Gomez rose up, scanning the room again. "Rita? Did you survive, *chiquita?"*

From the far side of the ruined room, just under the great gap where the windows had been, came a faint moan.

Crunching plastiglass fragments underfoot, avoiding stepping on anything that looked dangerous, he made his way closer to the sound. "Rita?"

"Aqui," she murmured.

"Okay, take it easy and I'll extricate you," he assured her. "You've got a goodly portion of the ceiling decorating you."

A small hand pushed free of the rubble. *"Gracias,"* she managed to say.

Gomez took the hand in his, bent and kissed it gently. Then he went to work.

ACROSS THE DARK waters of the lake you could see fires burning, more than a dozen of them, flaring up all across the city. Flames climbed high into the predawn sky.

"The pier looks to have survived," announced Gomez. "We can venture out onto it."

He and Rita were standing at its land edge. There were four medium-sized supply boats moored there, bobbing in the water.

The young woman glanced back at the ruins of the Detention Station. Her face was bruised, scribbled with lines of dried blood.

"There are others trapped in there," she said quietly. "I heard cries and groans while we were getting ourselves out, Gomez."

"So did I."

"Don't you think we ought to try to—"

"No, there's no time for that." He took hold of her arm. "Pretty soon some of the guards are going to be digging themselves out. And the secret police will be sending a rescue crew over here anytime now. None of them will hand us medals for being humanitarians—they'll just cut us down. We were prisoners, remember?"

"But there are other prisoners still trapped inside, lots of them. We can't just—"

"We have to leave or we'll get recaptured ourselves, *cara.*" He walked out onto the swaying pier, taking her along by the arm. "C'mon or we'll end up in worse shape than Dacobra."

"I think we must—"

"No, we're departing for elsewhere." Grunting, he scooped her up, carried her onto the nearest boat.

"What good does it do to believe in a just cause if you let people die?"

Setting her on the cabin floor, Gomez studied the control panel. "Ah, I can job this with no trouble," he decided.

"You're being an—"

"Listen, I saved your ass and mine tonight." He began fooling with the controls. "That's as far as it goes. Saving the other survivors of the quake is somebody else's responsibility."

"You're very cynical, Gomez." Folding her bruised, scratched arms, she backed against the cabin wall, frowning at him.

He got the engine going in under two minutes, pushed the automatic castoff button and started guiding the craft away from the island.

"Unfortunately," he said when they were aimed for Managua, "you met me about twenty years too late."

35

THE PRIVATE SKYLINER left Managua at a few minutes past two the next afternoon. Several of the quake-caused fires were still burning and the craft climbed through a rainy sky that was thick with sooty swirls of smoke.

Gomez, wearing one small bandage on his forehead and another on his cheek, was reclining in a very comfortable chair in Compartment A. "There's something to be said for wealth and influence," he observed.

Jake nodded in Bev's direction. "Thanks again for inviting us along." His left arm, from elbow to wrist, was enclosed in a plasticast.

She was seated near one of the oval windows, looking down at the retreating city. "Maxfield didn't say I couldn't invite a few friends along," she said. "I don't think any of you wanted to hang around Nicaragua just now."

Jake frowned. "Trouble is, most of the people responsible for the murders of Eve and Junior got killed off in the damned quake. It—"

"So did two hundred others," reminded Bev.

"I meant they can't be brought to justice."

"You have to rely on divine retribution sometimes," said Gomez. "Although there's a rumor that Dominic Hersh was defunct before his *casa* folded up on top of him and all his Tek gear."

Bev said, "They haven't found the remains of Izabel Morgana yet either."

"Her *hacienda* turned into a half acre of firstclass rubble during the twenty-six seconds of the quake," reminded Gomez. "After which it sank into a brand-new opening in the earth. An experience like that is *muy difícil* to walk away from."

"Yes, I know," admitted Bev. "But Dr. Morgana had reasons to disappear, since she must know we've found out what's going on."

"Want to go in on this pool, Jake? Is Izabel defunct or ain't she?"

"We know for certain that Dacobra and Hersh are finished," he said. "Her I'm not sure about."

Bev, turning away from the window, said, "I turned in a prelim report to Maxfield. I told him what I think really happened to his son and why. Until I hear otherwise, I'm assuming my job is finished."

"I contacted Bascom just before we took off," said Jake. "He wants us to keep on this."

"Until we put the Veep in the can?" Gomez rubbed at one of his bandages.

"Bascom suspects there might be gratuities and honorariums forthcoming from sundry enemies of Brookmeyer and McCracklin if we get the whole Surrogate 13 mess out in the open."

Bev said, "Maxfield will probably also be working to do that."

"Competition is the essence of the news business," Gomez pointed out.

"I'm going to head for Florida," said Jake, "and see about springing the *real* President Brookmeyer. Sid, the other angle on this is—"

"*Sí,* somebody's got to expose the android prez as a fraud." He smiled, nodding. "I'll handle that end of things, even though it means temporarily splitting up our crackerjack team, *amigo.*" He leaned further back in his seat. "Karla Maxfield is traveling with that Cracker Barrel gang and I imagine she'll be thrilled and elated to encounter me yet again. But, then, who wouldn't be?"

Bev mentioned, "You don't have much of a self-esteem problem, Gomez."

"Actually, I do, *cara.* I tend to underestimate my charm and abilities, but I understand there's a new capsule you can take to correct that."

Bev said to Jake, "Would you mind if I tagged along with you to Florida?"

"Not at all, but I thought we were rivals."

"I'm officially finished with my case, far as I can see. I'd like, though, to be in on the windup of this."

"Okay, fine."

"Milagro," murmured Gomez, "a miracle of cooperation."

RICHARD BASCOM SAID, "What?"

The polite voice of the apartment computer said, "I was suggesting, sir, that you might have given me a wrong command."

"Not that I know." He was sitting in the afternoon living room, wearing his pajamas and staring at a blanked window.

"But you requested that I *lower* the room temperature. Actually, however, it's quite low already and you're sitting there barefooted. In your present condition—"

"My condition happens to be okay," Richard said. "I'm fine, absolutely fine. When your wife dies that doesn't mean *you* get sick."

"A great many stressful things have been happening, sir," said the computer. "When we monitored your vital signs this morning, for instance, we found that—"

"Who in the hell told you to do that?"

"It's a standard procedure, sir. Every—"

"Well, forget about it," he said. "Now turn the room temp down. I'm roasting in here."

"Ought I to send for the building medibot?"

"Just go away, asshole."

A moment later, after making a sedate coughing noise, the computer told him, "There's a call for you."

"Not interested in calls."

"It's your father in Greater Los Angeles."

Richard sat up. "Okay, put him on—he must have some news about Eve."

Bascom, seated stiffly at his desk, flashed onto the wallscreen. "You're not looking well, son. Are you—"

"Don't you start in on me."

"I'm concerned about you, for Christ sake. You can't just—"

"Do you have news or not?"

"Yeah, the whole thing is pretty much solved," his father told him. "But you're going to have to promise not to try anything drastic."

"The hell I will." He got to his feet, glaring at the screen. "Who killed my wife? Who killed her, damn it?"

"This is a very tricky case," began Bascom. "When the details get out—well, there's going to be one hell of an upheaval. When that happens, and there's no doubt at all but that it will, everyone involved will be taken care of by the proper authorities."

"Oh, do they have proper authorities to take care of the murder of your wife? What kind of legalistic jargon are you trying to—"

"Hold it, back off. Calm down, sit in that goddamn chair and listen to me."

"Okay, but tell me something." He slumped down in the chair.

"The Surrogate 13 business involves President Brookmeyer, Vice President McCracklin and quite a few other folks here and there," began Bascom. He gave his son a concise account of just about everything Jake, Gomez and he himself had come up with since the start of the investigation into Eve Bascom's death. He concluded, "As you know, the youthful louts who did the actual killing are dead. Dominic Hersh is dead, too, probably knocked off by his own people. Captain Dacobra and Izabel Morgana are dead, too. Which means that just about every major figure in this is—"

"Just about, but far from *all,*" his son interrupted. "McCracklin had to be involved in the orders to kill my wife. What about him?"

"Soon as this comes out, the VP will face impeachment and a federal rap."

"No, somebody'll pardon him. They'll pull a shuffle and he'll end up with a fat job in some defense—"

"They won't," insisted his father. "Chiefly because most of them will be in the pokey, too, or looking for new sources of employment."

"I don't think that's the way things work."

"Be that as it may, I want you to let things run their course." Weariness was showing in Bascom's face. "Eve's death doesn't make much sense, but—"

"It makes perfect sense. She knew something important, so she had to be killed to keep her quiet."

"Anyway, it's over," said his father. "Let us take care of tying it all up."

Richard looked away from the image of his father. "Okay, yes, you're absolutely right," he conceded. "I really do appreciate all you've done. I'll call you again in a couple of days, when I'm feeling better."

"Take care." Bascom left the screen.

Richard said to the computer, "Find out where Vice President McCracklin is at the moment."

THE ROBOT ON the sundeck said, "Now your left hand, chum."

Bascom shifted the neowicker basket from his left hand to his right, scowling at the big battleship-grey mechanical man. "The prints will be the same as on my right hand, nitwit."

"You can comply, buddy, or I can administer a little shock that'll make your hair do a tapdance and your goonies go south."

Bascom sighed and complied.

Seven minutes later the guardbot accepted him as Walt Bascom and allowed him to enter the Zuma Sector beach house.

There was another guardbot in the blank-windowed living room with Kay Norwood. This one was white-enameled and took only three and a half minutes to establish that the agency head was who he said he was.

"Now I'll have to turn that basket over to the kitchen staff," said the bot. "They'll check it for poison and any other additions."

Handing him the basket, Bascom sat in an armchair facing the tall blonde lawyer's sofa. "I brought you a basket of fruit," he explained.

"Thanks—and some news?"

He nodded, asking, "Had any trouble here?"

"Well, outside of having a tough time getting used to living with a half dozen belligerent robots and not being able to enjoy the ocean view—no, I feel much safer here than I did under the Lighthouse. And nobody's tried to get at me."

"Within a couple more days you should be able to come out in the open again." He explained to her what Jake and Gomez had found out, what they'd been up to in Nicaragua and what they were planning to do next.

When he finished, Kay observed, "You don't look especially elated."

Bascom drummed the fingers of his right hand on his right knee. "I'm concerned about my son's reaction to all this," he admitted. "Fact is, and I don't like to do this, I put extra Manhattan operatives on him. These lads are to tail him and keep him from doing anything goofy."

"You mean in the way of revenge?"

"His wife was murdered and Richard feels, I'm near certain, that he *personally* has to do something."

"Most of the people involved in Eve's death are dead themselves."

"Not all of them, though. Not McCracklin, for instance."

Her eyes widened. "He wouldn't try to get at the vice president?"

"I really don't know."

"The people you have watching him will see that nothing serious happens."

Bascom stood. "Okay, I just wanted to fill you in on the current situation. I'll—"

"I was about to have some lunch," Kay said, standing. "Got time to join me?"

"I'll dampen your feast."

She smiled at him. "You can't be as bad as these robots."

Bascom hesitated before answering, "Okay."

36

□

GOMEZ'S LATEST RENTED skycar came without intrusive commercials. Whistling "Cielito Lindo" with his tongue pressed against his upper teeth, the curlyhaired detective was piloting it over the hills surrounding Chattanooga. Spotting his destination, he tapped out a landing pattern.

The skyblue cruiser dropped gracefully down through the sunny afternoon, settling to a gentle landing in a woodland clearing. At the far side of the glade stood a parked two-story mobile home. It was painted in camouflage colors.

When Gomez tried to disembark, he discovered his doors wouldn't open. "Hey, *que pasa?*"

The dash voxbox spoke. "Who the frak are you?"

"This is my own rental asking me that?"

"C'mon, c'mon, dimbulb, answer up."

"I'm Sid Gomez of the Cosmos Detective Agency. Is this Arlo Harmon?"

"Would Arlo Harmon go around with a voice like an aluminum cockatoo? Stop gabbing and answer the questions, huh? What's your business here?"

"I arranged a meeting with Harmon. I want to hire Cyberwacky Services, Ltd."

"What was the agreed on fee?"

"Two thousand dollars, which is a hell of a—"

"No, nope. You got that wrong, fella."

"I never get a fee wrong. I agreed to pay Cyberwacky the sum of—"

"It's 2,500 dollars in front," said the voxbox. "Otherwise, junior, you can fly your woebegone butt right on out of this sylvan setting."

Gomez leaned back in his seat, poking his tongue into his cheek. Narrowing his eyes, he looked out at the trees surrounding him. Most of them were real, mixed with only a few holoprojections. Finally he said, "Two thousand five hundred dollars it is. Provided Cyberwacky can do *exactly* what I have in mind."

"Cyberwacky Services, Ltd., can do any darn thing you can think of, dimwit. C'mon in, kiddo. And wipe your feet on the doormat."

The car let him get out.

DR. VINCENT CHEN said, "I suppose I do owe you a small favor, Jake."

His private office was large, with a wide window giving a view of a bright, secure section of the Miami Enclave. There was no desk and Jake was in an armchair facing the psychiatrist's armchair. "I need a fairly large one, Vince."

"When we were both cops in SoCal, you did . . . Excuse me a second." He picked up the lap phone from the floor beside him. "Yes? Dr. Chen here."

The phone had an earbug, so Jake didn't hear the other side of the conversation. He turned to watch a row of shimmering palm trees out on the street.

"His brain implant monitor ought to be functioning perfectly by now, Mrs. Henzler. . . . Suicidal? No, that's not a common side effect. . . . Yes, of course. Talk to Nurse Gallardo about getting him in to see me early next week. . . . I understand, yes, but we don't have a thing earlier. . . . Fine, goodbye." He dropped the phone to the floor. "Now, Jake, explain this to me."

"I have to get in and out of the Bergstrom Clinic," he said. "Safely."

"Very exclusive place, all kinds of tough security." Chen

rubbed his palm down across his face. "They run a . . . Excuse me a second. Hello? Dr. Chen here. . . . Moodjax should be helping you already, sir. . . . Suicidal? Well, maybe I better switch you to Calmtex. . . . No, I don't think you need an implanted monitor just yet. . . . I'll contact your drugbot. Better talk to Nurse Gallardo about coming in for a visit early next month. Right, bye." He frowned across at Jake. "Is this a criminal case you're working on?"

"In a way, yeah," he answered. "I also have to spring a patient out of there."

"Jesus, Jake—that's mighty near impossible."

"But not completely so, Vince."

"Give me some details, will you?"

"Sure," said Jake. "The President of the United States is being held there against his will while an android dupe of him is running the country."

Chen picked up the phone once more. "Nurse Gallardo," he requested, "hold all my calls."

ARLO HARMON WAS short, had crinkly brown hair and was forty-one. The parlor of his mobile home was a maze of gadgets, large and small, winking, blinking and humming. One wall was jammed with twenty-three small television screens, each tuned to a different channel.

Standing wide-legged, hands behind his back, the proprietor of Cyberwacky Services, Ltd., was scanning the screens. "You came while three of my favorite soaps are airing," he mentioned in his deep, chesty voice. *"Marriage on the Moon, Microsurgery Center* and *Love Among the Robots.* You follow any of 'em?"

"Not lately," admitted Gomez, who was leaning against the detached torso of a silvery robot. "Before I hand over this outrageous amount of dough, suppose—"

"I'm not in the mood for flapdoodle, Gomez," said Harmon, perching on the edge of a dictadesk. "Twenty-five hundred smackers is a mere spit in the deep blue sea to a topseed private eye outfit like yours. I'm fully aware of what a Cosmos expense account reads like, so—"

"Can you tear yourself away from this romantic gunk long enough to—"

"A guy who, according the the personality review I ran on you, watches air hockey games when he's—"

"Suppose we concentrate, the both of us, on the job at hand?"

Harmon pointed at the wall of screens. "There's your boy—third row, second screen from the left."

President Brookmeyer, or rather the Brookmeyer simulacrum, was up there grinning broadly. He was sitting, legs dangling, on the rail around the imitation train car he was traveling in.

Harmon pointed to another wall and a large vidscreen materialized. It provided a blowup of the presidential talk.

". . . fellow Americans, I just want to tell you how happy and delighted I am to get close to you all like this. You folks are the . . ."

"And similar guff, etcetera, etcetera." Harmon killed the sound. "He is the one you're interested in, isn't he? This second-rate android?"

Frowning, Gomez inquired, "How'd you find out he was a fake?"

When Harmon shook his head, his hair made faint crackling noises. "You're chinning with the CEO of Cyberwacky Services, Ltd., fella," he reminded. "I can't spot an andy at twenty paces? I can't find out what you and Cardigan have been up to in that shaky banana republic? I'm not six jumps and a couple of hops ahead of what you're contemplating in that coco of yours?"

"Do you know *why* I dropped in on you?"

"There you've got me, Gomez," admitted the electronics wizard. "I can make some nifty guesses, though. But tell me how we can serve you."

"The folks who touted you to me, Harmon, tell me that one of your specialties is remote control, telemetry and related areas."

"That's one of a multitude of our specialties, sure." He

glanced at all three of his soap operas for a moment. "Bam! I've got it, right on the noggin. You want me to take over that pitiful sim and—"

"Can you do it?"

"For 3,500 dollars."

"Wow, the inflation rate in these parts is something awful."

"We're talking a very tricky task here, dimwit."

"A thousand bucks more tricky?"

"That's a thousand skins in *front,*" corrected Harmon. "Plus, maybe you ought to jot these figures down so they don't slip out of your sconce, *plus* another two thousand bucks when it's over."

Gomez moved closer to the screens. He watched the imitation president speaking to a small crowd in Atlanta. "Okay. The Cracker Barrel Express will hit Chattanooga tonight at around sundown. Let me explain what, exactly, you're going to do for me."

"I've got a pretty fair idea already," said Harmon.

37

◨

NATHAN ANGER SAT up suddenly in bed, reaching for the lazgun beneath his pillow.

A metal hand caught his wrist. "Your nerves are really shot, Nate," said the silverplated robot.

"Why are you in my room? The deal is you don't—"

"I'm your *partner,*" Sunny reminded the OCO agent. "This is an emergency."

"What's an emergency?"

"Frank Dockert has a rush assignment for us."

Pushing the looming robot aside, Anger tumbled free of the bed. "How do you know what Dockert wants?"

"How else? We just talked on the phone."

"He's supposed to deal with me. That's the procedure we—"

"You should appreciate the fact that I just saved your butt, Nate," the big robot told him. "Rather than inform Frank that you were in here in the middle of the day sleeping off a hangover, I said you'd stepped out to—"

"I was working last night until six AM. That's the only reason—"

"You've got very spindly legs for a chubby man."

"I'm in no way chubby." Locating his trousers, Anger put them on. "Now what's this urgent damned assignment?"

"Sounds to me like a last chance sort of thing." Sunny settled into an armchair. "If you botch this one you'll be behind a desk in the bowels of DC from hence on."

Anger stopped in the doorway to the bathroom. "If I'm through, so are you."

"No, I'll simply team up with a better agent," said the robot. "Anyway, Nate, Dockert isn't happy with the way you screwed up the surveillance of Jake Cardigan while he was in Manhattan. Should you futz this new—"

"Tell me what the new assignment is, damn it."

"Jake Cardigan has been sighted in the Miami Enclave."

Anger said, "Then he must know about Brookmeyer."

"That's exactly what Dockert concludes," said Sunny. "Cardigan is to be discouraged from poking further into this business."

"How far can we go?"

The robot put his metal hands behind his head, eyed the ceiling and chuckled. "Far as we want to, Nate."

KARLA MAXFIELD CAME into the bedroom of her suite at the Atlanta Skytel and found Gomez, legs crossed, sitting on her unmade bed. She stopped just over the threshold, caught her breath and then squinted at him. "A very believable projection," she remarked. "How're you doing this?"

"It's merely—"

"Another innovation from Cyberwacky Services, Ltd.," put in a deep voice from an unseen source.

"Begone, Arlo," suggested Gomez. *"Buenas tardes,* Karla. How are you faring?"

"I'm fine and dandy. Where are you at the moment, Gomez?"

"Chattanooga, *cara."*

"We'll be there this evening. Want to meet for dinner?"

"An interesting and intriguing suggestion," said the holographic projection of the detective. "This, however, is more than just a social call. I wanted to make certain you'll be attending the Cracker Barrel speech here tonight."

Crossing the room, the young woman sat on the bed a few feet from his image. "Frankly, I was planning to skip it and just hit the press party afterward. It's the same darn speech he—"

"You don't want to miss this one," he advised.

"Oh, really?"

"When last we met, you mentioned a scandal involving the president that you were going to look into. Have you come up with anything, *chiquita?*"

"So far I've got somebody on Brookmeyer's staff just about persuaded to talk—and provide some pics—about the president's Tek habit," she answered. "I should be able to break that story in my . . . But, wait now." She leaned closer to the projected detective. "You've got something bigger than that, haven't you?"

"Considerably bigger, *sí.*"

"Is this exclusive to me? You haven't passed it on to that emaciated Newz reporter you hang out with?"

"This advance warning is exclusive," he told her. "After tonight, however, every reporter who's in attendance will have it. I wanted to make sure you didn't miss this, Karla."

"Okay, allright, I'll settle for that, I guess," she said, frowning. "Now what exactly have you got, *amigo?*"

Gomez filled her in on what he had and what he was planning for tonight in Chattanooga. "That's why I think you ought to drop in," he concluded.

"Oh, I shall." Karla smiled, hugging herself. "And I'll make certain my father's vidpeople attend, too."

"Bueno," said Gomez. "I want this story to spread rapidly around the globe."

"Oh, you can depend on that," she said. "And how about dinner afterward?"

"If I'm still extant, it's a date."

Karla kissed the cheek of his image just as it started to fade away.

38

◻

PART OF MIAMI Slum was ablaze. Huge clouds of smoke, sooty black and chalky white, were swirling up into the afternoon sky. Firevans were hooting as they raced there.

Jake blanked the windows of their Miami Enclave hotel suite. "Distracting," he said.

"Other people's tragedies usually are," said Bev.

Up on the vidwall of the large living room was a projected floor plan.

Jake returned to his chair, sitting on the arm. "Okay, this is Level 1 of the Bergstrom Clinic, based on data from Vince Chen and a select group of knowledgeable informants," he said. "There doesn't seem to be anyplace on that floor where President Brookmeyer can be stored."

Crossing to the wall, Bev tapped a portion of the detailed diagram. "Here's the Monitoring Room and the Security System Center, which look to be directly behind Dr. Bergstrom's personal office."

"Yep, so once we get into his hideaway, we can defuse the alarm setup," said Jake. "Let's look at Level 2."

The suite computer complied, shifting diagrams.

"Two possibilities here," suggested Bev. "Nobody seems to know what's in this big room right off the ramp entrance. And the tenant of this complex of rooms at the rear isn't known."

"They must have Brookmeyer monitored, so we may be able to find out once we get a look at the monitoring screens. Otherwise, we'll have to check both those possible locations."

Stretching up out of her chair, she said, "I'd better change into a more serious outfit, since I'm going to be your personal psychiatrist."

"I can probably pass for a Tek addict dressed just as I am," said Jake.

Saying nothing, Bev went into her bedroom.

Jake studied the plans of the two-story clinic again. He was still doing that when the door of the living room rattled, shimmered and then began to fall away to gritty grey dust.

THE CRACKER BARREL Express, consisting of five large landvans that had been modified to look like oldfashioned railroad passenger cars, was rolling along the highway toward Chattanooga. In the presidential car, which was midway in the procession of vans, Vice President McCracklin was tapping on the door of President Brookmeyer's private compartment.

The door was opened by a Secret Service agent, a large woman holding a lazpistol in her left hand. "Yes, Mr. Vice President?"

"I have to talk to President and Mrs. Brookmeyer."

"I'll see if—"

"Send Mac right on in, Mildred," ordered the president. "You wait out in the corridor for a spell, okay?"

"Very well, sir."

Trina Brookmeyer was a thin, blonde woman of fifty. She was sitting facing the Brookmeyer simulacrum. When the door shut, she asked, "Now what, schmuck?"

"Honey," suggested the android, "you ought not to address Mac that way, even in private. Afterall, he's the—"

"Is there any way to shut him off enroute?" she asked McCracklin. "It's difficult to believe, but I really believe he's an even *bigger* bore than Warren himself."

"Dear, that's no way to—"

"Just sit there," ordered McCracklin, "and shut the hell up."

The android frowned and squared his shoulders. "I should

think, Mac, that the dignity of my office would prevent you from—"

"Hush up," the First Lady told him.

"Very well. I bow to the majority opinion." The Brookmeyer dupe folded his arms and gazed out the one-way window. "Wonderful countryside this, makes you proud to be an American."

Trina patted the seat beside her. "Sit down and tell me what's bothering you," she invited. "You look worried."

Joining her, McCracklin said, "I don't think it's anything serious, Trina."

"You wouldn't look so green around the gills if it weren't damned serious. So what's wrong?"

"You already know about the mess down in Nicaragua. We—"

"I thought everyone who could talk was dead. Thanks to an act of god and some help from the Office of Clandestine Operations."

"That's more or less true, except we're still not certain about Dr. Izabel Morgana. Her body hasn't been found yet."

"I'm sure she's buried under a ton or so of adobe bricks."

"And Jake Cardigan is in the Miami Enclave, along with Bev Kendricks."

"Two aging excops." She gave him a look that conveyed disappointment with him. "I suppose you're also still worried about that greaser. Chavez, is it?"

"Gomez," corrected the vice president. "Sid Gomez. The fact of the matter is, he's dropped from sight and we have no idea where he's gotten to."

"Hopefully he fell into a deep hole in Managua."

"No, he's in the United States somewhere, but he's managed to dodge all our tails."

"I still fail to see why you worry about such an—"

"Those were cows," said Brookmeyer. "Not robot cows, but the real thing. You know, that's the sort of experience, the sort of simple, everyday sight, that makes a trip such as this one so darned—"

"Be still," the First Lady told the android. "You're much more uneasy than needbe, Mac."

"Perhaps we ought to cancel the speech in Chattanooga tonight," he suggested. "Announce that he's sick or—"

"I'm fit as a fiddle," said the Brookmeyer simulacrum. "I never felt better and I really believe it's this wonderful trip that's—"

"We'll certainly do tonight's speech," said Trina firmly. "We'll do *all* the rest of the speeches on our schedule. Then we'll take him back to DC and start running things in such a way that—"

"There's something else?"

"What now, Mac?"

"Well, I've gotten word from some of the Joaquim Tek Cartel people," said the vice president. "They're, obviously, not too happy about the way things went in Managua. More important, they think the president ought to start planting the idea that the penalties for Tek dealing and chip manufacture are much too harsh. They'd like that to begin showing up in his whistle-stop speeches and—"

"Tek is a scourge," said Brookmeyer. "It is my opinion that—"

"Quiet down," suggested Trina. "You tell those Joaquim bastards that we are going to do this *gradually.* First some government reports indicating the seriousness of the Tek danger has been overestimated and so on. *Then* Warren will start shifting his position."

"Joaquim paid for a goodly part of this whole—"

"They'll get back a lot more than they invested, but they are going to have to be *patient,"* she said. "Now, get back to this Cardigan problem. What's being done to take him out of play?"

"We've assigned Nathan Anger and his robot associate to work on this. He'll—"

"Anger's an incompetent buffoon. Your people aren't seriously—"

"Let me finish, Trina." He put a hand on her arm. "Anger, quite obviously, isn't aware of this and neither is Sunny. Sunny's the robot. The thing is, the robot has been modified."

"How?"

"This is an idea we've borrowed from the Tek people," continued McCracklin. "Sunny is now very similar to one of their kamikaze androids."

"When he gets near Cardigan, he'll explode?"

Nodding and smiling, the vice president said, "That's it exactly. We'll get rid not only of Cardigan and that robot, but of Anger and the Kendricks woman as well."

39

THE SILVERY ROBOT came striding into the living room of the suite first. "Try something cute, Cardigan," invited Sunny.

"You should've knocked." Jake was standing next to a straight chair, facing what had once been the door. "Less messy."

Nathan Anger sent dust scattering up as he followed in the wake of his robot partner. "Sunny's eager sometimes." He had his lazgun pointed at Jake. "Call Bev Kendricks in here, will you?"

"There's no need." She entered from her bedroom, still wearing the same clothes. "You've violated a whole stewpot of our rights already, Nathan."

"It won't read that way in our report," the OCO agent assured her.

"Armed resistance," amplified the robot. "It sounds foolish, but you two tried to shoot it out with us rather than answer a few routine questions. Sad and a pity." He chuckled.

Bev ignored him and nodded at the agent. "In a few hours, Nathan, just about all of the people you work for are going to be out of jobs and in deep trouble. Killing us won't—"

"This isn't merely duty," said Sunny, moving a step nearer to Jake. "There's a great deal of personal satisfaction involved."

Jake grinned. "Call him off, Nate," he advised.

"I'm sorry, Jake, but this is orders," said Anger.

"Orders from who?"

"I suppose it won't hurt to tell you that Frank Dockert authorized this."

"And Dockert gave the order to you directly?"

"Actually, Cardigan, he told me," said the robot. "I'm equally important in this—"

"From what I've been hearing, Nate, this bot of yours isn't any too reliable," Jake told the agent. "Any further screwups and it's off to the junkyard for Sunny."

"That's a damn lie!" The robot's voice rose.

"Are you even sure that Dockert gave any such order, Nate? Sunny's goofy enough to make up the whole—"

"Shut up, Cardigan," shouted the robot, taking another step toward him. "Shut your damn mouth!"

Jake shook his head, his grin widening. "Sunny, you're going to have to learn not to interrupt when your betters are talking."

"*Betters!*" Making an angry, growling noise, the silvery robot came charging at Jake.

Jake dropped to the floor, at the same time grabbing up the metal chair.

He thrust the chair up as the mechanical man dove for him. The legs of the chair hit the robot in the chest and, using the chair as a lever, Jake sent him sailing across the room.

Sunny hit a window, hard. The glass cracked and he went flying clean out of the room and into the smoky afternoon.

Anger started running toward the window.

But before he reached it, there was an enormous explosion from outside.

Slowing, Anger moved carefully to the jagged gap and stared down. "Sweet Jesus," he said very quietly, "they had him loaded with explosives."

"Turned him into a kamikaze," said Jake, "to kill me."

"Yes, but . . . but if he'd gone off in this room. . . ." The agent's gun hand fell to his side and he suddenly sucked in a rasping breath. "I'd have been killed, too."

Jake said, "That's one hell of a retirement policy you guys have."

☐

GOMEZ WAS IN possession of very impressive and completely believable credentials, which identified him as an ace reporter for CarNet News. The guardbot at the press entrance to the Chattanooga Town Hall gave him a cordial bow as he returned the ID packet. "Glad to have you with us this evening, Mr. Silvera."

"I'm looking forward to a real treat." Smiling, Gomez tucked the spurious identification materials inside his jacket.

The meeting hall was meant to seat six hundred people. There were over a hundred media reporters inside the place already, overflowing the press section.

Karla Maxfield caught Gomez's eye and waved at him.

He returned the wave, pushing his way through the growing crowd of newspeople until he reached the row of seats where she was. *"Buenas noches,"* he said, halting in the aisle.

"Take a hike for yourself," suggested Norm, her bodyguard, who was jammed into the seat next to her.

"Norman, dear, scoot," ordered Karla. "I want Gomez next to me."

"A mistake."

"Be that as it may—vacate."

Giving a snorting, head shaking sigh, the big black man rose. "Don't try to paw the lady," he warned the detective.

"Tell her not to paw me," responded Gomez. *"I'm* the one who's irresistible." He settled into the surrendered seat. "You passed the word around that something was afoot, I notice, *cara."*

"Without spilling too many details, I notified a few people that this would be an interesting evening." She smiled, touching his hand. "Is everything going as planned?"

"Arlo Harmon of Cyberwacky Services, Ltd., swears that all is going well." Shoulders slightly hunched, he glanced around the hall.

The sound of shuffling feet and quiet conversations was drifting in from the rear of the hall as the doors opened to admit the audience.

"What do they pay you at Cosmos?"

"About half what I'm truly worth."

"Well, actually, I know. I had some people run a check on—"

"Remind me to invite you to my next seminar on privacy."

"Hey, listen, I'm interested in you, Gomez," she told him. "I admit that I thought you were a repellent and arrogant toad when we first bumped into each other, but that was simply because I'd allowed all the rotten reports I'd heard about your activities color my judgment. Once I started—"

"No need to apologize," he told her, patting the hand that was resting on his elbow. "Few people can resist the full force of the Gomez personality once they're exposed to it at close range for more than a few minutes."

She asked, leaning closer to him, "You won't come to work for me?"

"You're feeling warmhearted toward me because I chanced to save your life recently *and* I gave you a tip about tonight's festivities," he explained to her. "After a while, were I to become an employee of *Gossip Digest* and other Maxfield enterprises, you'd soon realize that I'm still the iconoclastic heathen you've always heard I was."

"Still, it would be fun for—"

"Fun mayhap, but completely out of the question."

She leaned back in her seat, looking toward the empty stage. "You're married, aren't you?"

"Surely your fact finders found that fact."

"You're currently married. But then, you've been married several times and they never seem to last."

"I'm still trying to get the hang of it."

"You're happily married this time?"

"I am, *si.*"

"But you never talk about your wife."

"All the more proof, *bonita,* that I am contentedly married," he said. "If I were—*Dios mio!*" He jumped to his feet.

"What's wrong?"

"Richard Bascom just came in. He's with the other civilians and is in the act of dropping into a seat across the hall."

"Your boss's son? What in the hell is he doing here?"

"Excuse me while I rush over and find out." He started working his way through the crowd in the aisle.

40

◻

HANDS UNDER HER armpits, Gomez lifted the small whitehaired woman out of her seat and deposited her in the aisle. "I'll only require your seat for a few moments, *mama grande,*" he assured her as he assumed her place. "Official business."

"Hey, you can't treat that old lady like that." A large man in the next row behind scowled at Gomez.

Ignoring him, the detective took hold of Richard Bascom by the arm. "Now that I'm seated beside you, Ricardo, suppose you tell what in blazes you're up to. I thought your pop had people keeping an eye on you."

"I ditched them, Gomez. And, as far as you're concerned, I don't need you either."

"Your *padre* gave you a report on what's behind all this, did he?"

"Yes, I know who was responsible for Eve's death."

"I'd really like my seat back, young man."

"*Momentito,* I swear," promised Gomez. "It's essential that I talk to this fellow."

"There's nothing to talk about. Leave me alone."

"Listen to me." His grip tightened. "I figure you're here looking to revenge yourself on McCracklin and—"

"You guys let all people responsible in Central America get away. I don't intend—"

"*Ay, Dios.* The earth opened and swallowed them. That's not exactly negligence on our part."

"McCracklin'll be on the stage any minute now."

"What're you going to do? You couldn't have sneaked a gun by the guardbots on the doors."

"I just have to get my hands on the bastard. I can—"

Gomez said, "You have to attend to what I'm saying, Richard. We've got something in the works that'll take care of him, take care of all of them."

"I don't want him taken care of, Gomez. I want to see him dead."

"You're not going to try anything." Glancing at the impatient woman in the aisle, Gomez punched Richard in the ribs.

As he doubled over in pain, Gomez dealt a quick, sharp side-hand blow to his neck.

Moaning, sighing out a breath, Richard slumped back in his seat and passed out.

Gomez hopped up. "Gracious, this poor man's had some sort of seizure."

"You slugged the poor boy," accused the whitehaired woman. "I saw you do it."

"Me? No, I happen to be this unfortunate lad's personal therapist. I've been trying to persuade him to come back with me to the rest home."

The big man in the next row said, "I saw you smack the poor sod."

"Lend me a hand," Gomez requested of him. "We'll have to carry him into the foyer for—"

"Ladies and gentlemen," announced the overhead speakers, "the President of the United States."

THE PRESIDENT OF the United States got up off his cot, legs a little shaky.

A panel in the grey wall had come whispering open.

"Well, finally," said Brookmeyer. "Somebody to get me out of this damned hole."

Nathan Anger took a few tentative steps into the small grey room. "I guess you could look at it in that way, sir."

"What do you mean? I assume this is an OCO operation to rescue—"

"Not exactly," said Jake, entering behind Anger.

"Who's this man, Agent Anger?"

"Jake Cardigan," said Jake. "If you'll come along with—"

"Cardigan?" The black president's frown deepened. "I've heard something about you, haven't I?" He rubbed at his forehead. "Isn't this man's name on one of your Office of Clandestine Operations shitlists, Agent Anger? I'm almost certain he—"

"I'm not exactly with the OCO, sir," said Anger, backing against the grey wall. "I've more or less resigned, but I pretended to be an agent still so that Cardigan and I could get in here safely."

"My original plan for accessing you didn't seem like it was going to work any longer," explained Jake. "Not after the OCO tried to assassinate me and Bev Kendricks and screwed it up in a pretty flamboyant way."

"They tried to kill me, too," added Anger. "They destroyed my partner."

"I'm not following this," said the president. "You're implying that the OCO is behind my being here and not—"

"How the hell do you think McCracklin's been able to pull all this off, sir? Of course, the top people in the OCO are in cahoots with him."

President Brookmeyer lowered himself to the cot and sat. "This is even more serious than I thought," he said. "You've got to get me to DC at once."

Jake grinned at him. "You're going to have to wait awhile."

"I don't intend to wait, Cardigan." The president stood up again. "Our country is in profound trouble. There's been an attempt at what amounts to a coup. If America, if this nation, is to survive, I must return to the helm as soon as possible."

Anger coughed into his hand. "The media," he said quietly.

"We'll control them, there's no need for the more unsettling details of all this ever to reach the public or—"

"Any time now," mentioned Jake, "the media will be descending on this clinic."

Brookmeyer nodded, unhappy, at Anger. "Did you alert them that I was here?"

Jake said, "You did."

"How could I possibly have—"

"Actually it's your android dupe," he said. "He ought to be doing that just about now down in Chattanooga."

UP ON THE stage the President Brookmeyer android stood surveying the audience. "Folks, I'm not going to deliver my regular speech this evening," he began. "What I have to tell you isn't pleasant, but I believe it's important that the American people know the truth."

Gomez was in the aisle, leaning against the wall. The white-haired woman had regained her seat and Richard was still slumped unconscious in his. A satisfied smile showed on the detective's face.

"Let me begin by saying, my fellow Americans, that I am *not* Warren Brookmeyer."

Murmuring got going in the audience.

"No, I am a cleverly constructed android simulacrum," continued the android, "constructed so that the administration could pull a fast one on you." As he spoke, the Brookmeyer dupe shrugged free of his coat. "Just so they won't try to cover up by claiming I'm simply suffering from delusions, I'll prove to you right now that I'm nothing more than a highly sophisticated mechanism." He got out of his shirt and singlet.

Most of the spectators were standing, staring at the stage. The level of murmuring and mumbling had risen.

"There, you can see my inner workings now." The android had opened a panel in his chest to reveal circuitry, beads of light and intricate twists of multicolored wiring. "Why, you well may ask, have I been traveling this great land of ours impersonating the chief executive? The answer, my friends, is simple—or at least it started out simple. Your real president, a man you all trusted, is a hopeless Tek addict and at this moment is a patient at the noted Bergstrom Clinic in the Miami Enclave."

Many of the reporters had left their seats to surge closer to the stage.

The Brookmeyer android continued, "I was, I ruefully admit, part of this shameful scheme. They wanted to lull you, the American public, into thinking that all was well while, in fact, your president was trying to cure his disgraceful addiction to Tek. You were meant to believe that I was the president and to suspect nothing."

"Bueno," said Gomez, arms folded and beaming. "Arlo Harmon of Cyberwacky Services, Ltd., is doing an *espléndido* job of controlling this expensive andy from afar."

"My friends, you haven't heard the worst of it," said the bare-chested android. "No, because even your once respected president wasn't aware of the *true* plot that was afoot. His once trustworthy vice president, James S. McCracklin, had conspired with—"

"That's enough!" McCracklin, a lazgun in his hand, came running out onto the stage. "Shut up, damn you!"

"This man," said the android, pointing an accusing finger, "this man, ladies and gentlemen, conspired with seemingly respectable members of government intelligence agencies and, worse, with vicious Teklords to—"

McCracklin fired at him.

The pulsing beam of the lazgun dug across the android's left side, cutting a jagged gap.

The Brookmeyer simulacrum staggered, swayed, brought a hand up to the smoking hole in his side. "My fellow Americans . . ." He toppled to his knees, fell forward, his head smacking the planking. He stretched out, twitching violently, went rolling off the stage to fall at the feet of the shouting reporters.

Rushing to the stage edge, McCracklin aimed his lazgun to fire again.

But before he could do that a Secret Service agent in the far aisle, looking somewhat confused, decided to use his stungun on the vice president.

McCracklin straightened up, arms swinging, feet dancing a few wobbly steps backward. He bumped into two more Secret Service agents who were rushing onto the stage and collapsed against them.

Nodding, Gomez reached across the whitehaired woman, giving her an apologetic smile. He tapped Richard, who was just coming to, on the shoulder. "You're going to have to settle for this," he told him. "And, as revenge goes, it ain't that bad."

41

□

BASCOM WAS SUBDUED, but somewhat less rumpled than usual. "As I anticipated," he was telling Gomez and Jake as he prowled his tower office, "certain parties have passed along some cumshaw. We picked up a few bonuses from folks who are pleased with the results of this investigation."

"This would be folks who are delighted to see McCracklin facing a long stay in the Freezer?" inquired Gomez, who was slouched in an armchair. "Plus those who are jolly about the possible impeachment of the real President Brookmeyer?"

"That sort of folks, exactly, yes," answered the head of the detective agency.

Jake was standing near a window, his back to the fading day outside. "We're sharing in this jackpot?"

"Of course, obviously. You'll find your Banx accounts have swollen handsomely."

"Your ideas of handsome, *jefe,* have often matched my notions of downright ugly in the past."

"Gomez, I have mellowed," he assured him. "Never again will I be considered a skinflint by my employees."

"I notice your suit isn't wrinkled," mentioned Gomez.

"Yet another turn for the better."

Jake asked, "What about your son?"

Returning slowly to his desk, Bascom sat down. "He's doing, I hear, pretty well."

"Back in Manhattan?"

"That's what I hear."

"Aren't you talking directly to Richard?"

"Well, he seems to feel I didn't handle the investigation into Eve's murder properly," Bascom admitted. "For now—I have to settle for having some New York ops keep an eye on him for me."

"I don't think he'll make any more tries to get revenge," said Gomez.

"No, that's passed, but he's still angry and unhappy."

"Takes a long time," said Jake, "to get over a death like that."

"I know, but I was hoping he'd realize that I . . . Well, I suppose we're not any further apart than we were when the whole mess started." Sighing, he stood up. "Gents, I must ask you to depart now."

"You're not planning to work late into the night?" asked Jake.

"I happen to have a dinner engagement."

Gomez bounced to his feet. "With a *señorita,* I bet. That accounts for the suit."

"Matter of fact, it's with Kay Norwood," said Bascom. "She's an interesting woman."

"She'd have to be." Gomez headed for the doorway. *"Vamanos,* Jake."

Jake nodded at the chief, grinning, and followed his partner out of the office.

JAKE'S SON POINTED his thumb at the vidwall. "You and Gomez really started things rolling," he said. "Seven resignations at the OCO today so far, five separate investigations in DC, three suicides. It's great."

"And, for those of us who thought that democracy still worked, a little unsettling." Jake took off his jacket and tossed it on a chair in their living room.

"I guess so, but still it is *fun* to watch things fall apart," said Dan, smiling at his father. "While you were over at Cosmos, Alicia Bower called a couple times. Three actually."

"Okay." He walked toward the deck, watching the night ocean.

"Are you, you know, involved with her?"

"No more than I was before."

"She told me you saved her life again."

Still looking out at the dark Pacific, Jake said, "I did that, yeah. But that doesn't mean we're engaged."

"You still haven't filled me in completely," his son reminded him, "on all that happened on this case."

The vidphone sounded.

Moving over to it, Jake answered. Then said, "Evening, Alicia."

"I'm home, back in Greater LA," the auburnhaired young woman told him. "Since you are, too, I want to suggest that we get together."

"Good suggestion, but not tonight."

"I've been watching Newz most of the afternoon," she said. "The whole country's going flooey. It's wonderful."

"That's what my son was saying."

Alicia hesitated. "You don't seem as elated as you ought to be."

"There's usually a letdown after a case is finished."

"I thought maybe—Well, there's something I better tell you," she said. "Don't get angry or anything. If I'd known what was going to happen to me, I would've spared myself the trouble."

"You're going to confess that those two goons who pretended to jump you the other night on the beach were indeed hired by you," Jake said. "I knew that already."

"You did?"

"Wasn't too difficult to figure out, or to check on," he said. "Remember what I told you at the time, Alicia, you don't need any excuse to contact me."

"Yes, I understand that now," she said. "I still get a little goofy at times. That's not why you're avoiding me?"

"We're friends, that's permanent," he assured her. "I like you and we'll continue to see each other. Tonight, though, I am on the brink of turning in."

"Allright, okay." She gave him a shy smile. "Goodnight, Jake."

As Jake moved away from the phone, his son said, "Sounds like you really aren't tangled up with her."

"Impressive piece of deduction."

The vidphone buzzed again.

This time it was Bev Kendricks. "Sorry, but I'm going to be at least a half hour late, Jake," the blonde detective said.

"Any trouble?"

"No, not at all. What's happening is that I'm trying to handle the new business that's starting to come in," she said. "It turns out that the notoriety I got from working with you on the Brookmeyer mess is helping my agency a lot."

"Only one of the many benefits," he said. "I'll meet you at the restaurant, Bev."

As his father left the phone, Dan said, "You didn't exactly give Alicia Bower a straight story, did you?"

"Not exactly, no."

"In fact, you lied."

"I still do that on occasion." Jake put a hand on his son's shoulder. "It turns out that sometimes the truth can cause all sorts of trouble."